STORIES

ROBERT PLANT

INDIES UNITED PUBLISHING HOUSE, LLC
P.O. BOX 3071
QUINCY, IL 62305-3071
www.indiesunited.net

For Dad

Table of Contents

"The universe is under no obligation to make sense to you."

-Neil DeGrasse Tyson

THE
PERFECT
MATCH

The Perfect Match

GRAND PRIZE WINNER OF THE SMALL BITES
SHORT STORY CONTEST

Alex was being followed. In fact, everywhere he went and everything he did was tracked down to the minute detail. The coffee he purchased in the morning sent data to several companies that utilize the information to push advertisements and help market their products. The same purchase that fueled his day also fueled these companies with large amounts of data at their disposal. That was how it worked, but it really only scratched the surface.

Now, they had access to his microphone. They could hear his conversations—who he talked to and about what topics. Nothing was off limits. His device worked for him, but it also worked against him by taking away his privacy. They even knew how many times a day he went to the bathroom. They knew what books he read, the movies he watched every Sunday night, and of course, the porn he watched on his phone before bed. Alex believed incognito mode protected him there, but these companies had ways around that.

They also knew Alex had moved to a new city in a new state. He needed a change of pace after striking out with countless women and feeling down on his luck. He thought this change would open up new doors for him. He moved to a college town where there were a ton of possibilities to meet women. Alex hadn't gone to college and worked in retail sales. It wasn't that he wasn't smart enough; he didn't have the drive. He wasn't motivated by money or social status. All he wanted was to meet a nice girl, date her for a while to ensure she was the right fit, ask her to marry him, and then have a dozen kids. In the end, all he wanted was the girl. Someone to love him and hold him like his mother used to when he was a child.

He sat at the bar with his right leg shaking in a

nervous twitch, sipping on his Jack and Coke. The flow of customers was steady considering it was a Friday night in a college town. There were patrons all around him, laughing and having a great time, but he sat alone waiting for his friend to join him. He pulled out his phone out of boredom with no one to talk to. He opened his dating app, Konnection, to check his messages, but the little red bubble popped up with only one message. It was from the admin of the app encouraging him to update some information on his profile. He laid the phone on the bar, but before he did, his new device took note of a few things.

First, it knew his location and even marked what stool he sat on at the bar. It used the microphone to record his drink order, and the front camera took note of the shirt he wore and how he styled his hair for the evening.

A young lady with honey hair that curled down past her shoulders walked into the bar in a hurry. She looked rushed, like she wanted to get a drink in before heading home to study for an exam. Alex blushed as she took the seat next to him while she fumbled through her oversized purse for her wallet. Unfortunately, as soon as she looked up to see him staring back at her, she moved over a few seats to keep her distance from him. She was way out of his league, and he drowned himself in his whiskey once he realized he didn't have a shot.

Maybe it was the little bit of acne he had growing on his right cheek. Maybe she could sense he didn't have any confidence in himself—most women could smell that on a man. Or maybe his wide-framed glasses and hunched posture turned her off. He had no way of knowing, and he wasn't about to ask her.

"Dude!" Alex's friend Noah screamed from across the bar. He walked through the crowd and slapped Alex on the shoulder. "What's goin' on, my man?"

"Not much."

Noah loosened the scarf around his neck and wiped the snow off his shoulders. He brushed his hands through his dark hair in James Dean fashion. He had the looks of James Dean, and his confidence came off like Sinatra, especially with his dark hair pulled back. Regardless, the ladies loved it, and they loved him. The way he conducted himself and the air of confidence he brought into a room every time he walked through the door.

"Did I just see you strike out? *Again*?" Noah motioned to the bartender. "I'll have a rum and Coke."

"No, you jackass. I didn't even say anything to her."

"Well, I saw her change seats and look at you like you're the Grim Reaper. We gotta get you laid tonight."

Alex sipped his drink without saying anything, either out of embarrassment or frustration. Maybe both.

"I mean, look at all these beautiful women around here." Noah waved his arms around, gesturing to several different groups of women, some of whom took notice. There was that air of confidence fogging up the room. "Aren't you glad you finally decided to move out here with your best bud?"

Alex nodded his head in agreement and sipped his drink.

The woman who had moved a few seats down gazed over at Noah and smiled. She sipped her rose-colored wine and turned toward the door, putting her back toward him.

"Watch this," Noah whispered into Alex's ear as he stood up from his stool.

Alex could hear mumbles of them talking under the tone of the crowd in the bar, but he couldn't make out exactly what they were saying. Within a minute, Noah had his arm around her, and they were laughing while they clinked their drinks together. It was like they had been friends for years. Alex couldn't understand how Noah could turn a complete stranger into someone who adored him after barely even knowing them. He did it all the time, and it drove Alex crazy.

He decided to ignore them and watch the baseball game on the television directly in front of him. The batter on the screen struck out, and Alex knew how he felt.

Noah came back after a few minutes and put his arm around Alex. "Alright, man. This is your chance. My new friend Mary over there has a friend for you. Don't fuck this up."

Alex glanced over and saw a somewhat pretty woman with natural features sitting next to the girl who had dissed him earlier and was now giving Noah "fuck me" eyes. This new girl looked like someone on his level, and he thought he might actually have a chance.

They all hung out, taking shots and telling stories, which mostly came from Noah. He could hold the attention of a room no matter the circumstances, and both girls seemed to eat it up. Alex's awkwardness got the best of him, and he had a hard time connecting with Mary's friend Amber.

Every movie Alex brought up, she hated. He loved meat; she was a vegan. He liked to play the popular, yet very nerdy, board game Dragons and Dwarves, but she hadn't even heard of the game. While Noah and Mary had their hands all over each other giggling every other second, Alex and Amber looked like two sore thumbs sitting across from each other.

By the end of the night, Noah went home with Mary, and Alex went home alone. Amber was very sweet and let him down easy, but it still burned at him that he couldn't make a connection with her.

Alex opened his phone in bed later that night, hoping to see a message in his Konnection app, but it read, "No New Messages." He closed his phone and looked up at the ceiling, feeling the room spin from the alcohol. His eyes fluttered closed as he went off to dream about his future life with a beautiful wife and kids running around their house. Despite being alone that night, he slept with a smile—although, he wasn't *really* alone. His phone was always with him. Always watching.

01000100 01100001 01110010 01101011 00100000 01001101 01100001 01110100 01110100 01100101 01110010

His phone buzzed on his nightstand early the next morning like it was telling Alex he needed to wake up and start playing with it. It was like a little kid waking up his parents to play, but really, it was Noah asking him to meet him at the diner for breakfast. Still, his phone had plenty to track that morning—how long he slept, the news articles he read while brushing his teeth, what clothes he put on for the day, what music he listened to while he walked to the diner, and what route he walked.

It wasn't only his phone doing the tracking. Security cameras on the street observed who he made eye contact with, what stores drew his attention, and what ads he took note of during his walk. Almost everything about this young man's life was tracked by the technology around him, right down to his watch recording each and every heartbeat he had.

Alex located his friend sitting in a booth at the back of the diner. The waitress refilled Noah's coffee, and Alex asked for one as well.

"Sup?" Noah's voice was low and worn out.

"Late night?"

"You could say that. I haven't slept."

"Must've been a good night with that girl you met then."

"Correction. *Girls*."

"No way! How?"

Noah wore sunglasses to help wane his hangover, and he tipped them down to look Alex right in the eyes. "You. All thanks to you."

"Pff. What?!"

"Yeah, that other girl ended up being her roommate. You struck out with her pretty hard, and she was jealous of her friend. I was able to spread the love though. If you know what I mean." As he said it, Noah spread jam across his toast. "Sorry for already ordering. I'm starving."

"I bet." Jealousy overtook Alex and he looked away depressingly. *Why is Noah so lucky with girls? Why was he born with his good looks?* Envy crept into his thoughts.

"Look." Noah cut into his stack of pancakes as he talked. "You're not gonna meet girls at bars, Alex. You read books. You watch old episodes of *The Twilight Zone* and *Star Trek*. Girls who are into that kinda stuff aren't going to be available for pickup at a bar. Those girls want a bad boy who drives a muscle car or a motorcycle."

"You think you're a bad boy? You don't drive a muscle car or have a motorcycle."

"Yeah, but I have good looks so I can get away with it."

Alex rolled his eyes at that one. "Alright, hot shot. Where am I going to meet girls that are more my speed then?"

Right as he finished his sentence, Alex's phone flashed an alert onto his lock screen—it was an email from a new dating app. Perfect Match promised Alex they'd found his soulmate. There were dozens of girls who were already interested in dating him, according to the email.

"What the hell?" Alex mumbled under his breath. He wondered how these girls knew who he was or anything about him.

"What? What is it?" Noah shoved a huge pile of pancakes into his mouth.

Alex ignored him and kept reading the email. Profile pictures and notes from different girls made up the rest of the email, and Alex's skepticism melted away. For example, one of the messages said she also loved *Star Trek* and *The Twilight Zone*. Alex thought it was a strange coincidence they were talking about those shows only a moment ago.

"If you don't tell me what the hell you're looking at, I'm gonna throw the rest of my pancakes at you."

"Have you heard of this new dating app, Perfect Match?"

"Nope." Noah became agitated at Alex for answering his question with another question.

"Well, this email is saying there are dozens of girls who are interested in me. I have no idea how they found out anything about me, though. This girl wrote to me saying she likes *The Twilight Zone* and *Star Trek*. We were just talking about that. Isn't that crazy?"

"Sounds like you struck gold, my man! You gotta write her back. Is she hot?"

"She's attractive for sure." Alex turned his phone to show Noah her picture. "Looks like she's way out of my league."

In fact, all the girls featured in the email looked out of his league. Most of them with wavy, blonde hair running past their shoulders and sparkling eyes gleaming at the camera. Not only were they all attractive, but they also had the same interests as Alex. Especially one girl, Jessica. She looked stunning, and her blue eyes locked on Alex's like a painting that follows you with its eyes when you walk by it in a haunted house.

"You should write her back. That Konnection app sucks, and you haven't had much success at the bars."

"I dunno, man. This seems...weird. Like it's too good to be true."

"If I were you, I'd give it a shot. You gotta keep putting yourself out there, or you're gonna end up an old lump of clay sitting in your recliner watching *Star Trek* reruns."

Alex thought about how everything always fell into Noah's lap. He always got what he wanted. Maybe this time the universe was turning things around in his favor. Maybe it was his turn to have something fall into *his* lap.

01000100 01100001 01110010 01101011 00100000 01001101 01100001 01110100 01110100 01100101 01110010

What were the chances the first girl he met on this app would end up being the one? It had only been a few weeks, and they were texting each other constantly. She knew *everything* about *Star Trek*. She even knew about the unaired pilot where Captain Pike was actually at the helm of the Enterprise. What beautiful 24-year-old girl knew about that? He was infatuated with her. Every free second he had in his day was dedicated to texting Jessica.

Alex: where have you been all my life?

Jessica: right here. waiting for you.

Alex: it's hard to believe you don't have a boyfriend. what am i missing?

Jessica: i have very specific taste Alex. i'm not looking for some fling either. i want to find someone real. i want to live long and prosper with someone :)

Alex: you could have any guy you want. why me? what makes me so special?

Jessica: you're adorable. plus i'm not completely sold on you…yet.

Alex: maybe i can change that. let's meet in

person. coffee tomorrow morning?

Jessica: coffee…that's boring. how about dinner? i know a really good place.

Jumping straight to dinner seemed aggressive to Alex, even though they'd already been talking for a few weeks. He had seen this play by girls on these apps in the past and had been burned. He would take them out to this fancy dinner, they'd stumble through awkward conversations, he'd pay the bill, and he'd never hear from them again. Ghosted.

Despite his reservations about joining the app and now dinner, he felt drawn to Jessica. He had this feeling in the pit of his stomach that made him anxious but in a good way. Something he'd never felt before. Maybe it was the beginning of something special, and it scared him a little bit.

All he knew was he was sick of being alone, and it was time to make a change.

01000100 01100001 01110010 01101011 00100000 01001101 01100001 01110100 01110100 01100101 01110010

Alex stood outside the restaurant, waiting for Jessica to arrive, with his hands fidgeting inside his pockets. He had never been this nervous for a date in his life. Looking at the place from the outside even intimidated him. He didn't even think he could afford to eat at a place like this.

Jessica pulled up in her car—a smooth-looking Lexus—while Alex had walked because he didn't even have a car. There wasn't a need for one in the city really, but still, he felt diminished knowing she drove a car probably worth more than he made in a year. He wondered how a young girl in her twenties could even afford a car like that. Maybe her parents were rich.

Jessica popped out of the driver seat, closed the door, and smiled from ear to ear as she walked up to Alex.

"Wow!" Alex's jaw almost dropped to the ground.

"Are you referring to my dress or the car?" Jessica twirled in a circle creating a flow on the skirt of her dress that would hypnotize almost any man.

"Would you be upset if I said both?"

"Ha! You're so adorable." Jessica leaned in and gave him a kiss on his cheek. She stayed close to his face, peering into his eyes, trying to hypnotize him in case the skirt didn't do the trick.

Alex's face flushed, and he awkwardly glanced over to the door of the restaurant. "I probably shouldn't say this...but I dunno if I can afford this place."

"Who said you were buying? C'mon." She grabbed his hand and pulled him to the door where he graciously opened it for her. She curtsied at him. "Aw, thank you. Such a gentleman."

They walked up to the concierge, and Jessica gave the hostess her name for the reservation.

"Is it just me or wouldn't it be so cool if all

doors made the same sound from *Star Trek*?" Jessica mimicked the futuristic swoosh of a door opening and closing like the show. It almost sounded perfect to Alex like she had a recording of the sound playing from her mouth.

"I was just saying that to my friend the other day!"

"No way!" She gently slapped him on the shoulder and proceeded to cuddle into it while they waited for their table to be ready. It was like this was their hundredth date, not their first. They had an instant connection, and it seemed like Jessica didn't want to let go of Alex. It was a dream for him to have this beautiful girl all over him. His tensions loosened, and he soaked in everything about her. How her hair glistened in the light with every turn of her head. The way she smiled out of the corner of her mouth. Those blue eyes pierced his soul every time she looked at him.

While Jessica leaned against his shoulder, Alex reached down and pinched his arm.

"What was that?" She pulled back confused.

"I had to pinch myself to make sure I wasn't dreaming."

Jessica immediately grabbed him by the back of the head and kissed him on the lips. It was a gentle kiss with only a little bit of tongue. It surprised Alex, but once his brain comprehended what was happening, he sunk into her and kissed her back. Usually, this happened at the end of a date. Well, not for Alex, but that was what he saw in the movies.

They were seated in the back of the restaurant with dimmed lighting and a view of the ocean behind the restaurant. It was the best seat in the house. Alex picked up the menu and noticed the prices.

"Okay...I really can't afford this."

"I told you this is on me. You're a chivalrous guy, Alex, but I also know you're not egotistical enough to let this bother you. Besides, who's to say which gender should purchase the meal on a first date."

"In that case, I'll have the steak and lobster."

Jessica boomed out a raucous laugh. "You are so funny I can't stand it. Just make sure you leave room for dessert." She winked at him, making it seem like she wasn't talking about food.

Most men would insist on paying, but she knew Alex was easily persuaded. In fact, that was one of the main traits she had honed in on when reviewing his profile. She knew she could manipulate him and get him to do whatever she pleased. Jessica wasn't hungry and decided to push things forward a little more quickly than anticipated. Usually, she'd at least allow the courtesy of one last meal for her candidates but not tonight. She was under orders to get the job done as quickly as possible.

They both continued to look at the menu, but Jessica's eyes sharply peered over her menu at Alex. She placed her menu down on the table as the waiter approached.

"Good evening." The waiter stood at their table with his hands behind his back. "Welcome to the..."

"I'm sorry, but may we please have another minute."

The waiter nodded and walked off.

Jessica leaned across the table displaying her well-rounded breasts to Alex as she tucked her hair behind her ear. "Let's get outta here."

"What? Really? I thought this was going well, no?" Alex immediately thought he had blown the date already.

"It is...I just thought we could maybe have more fun back at my place. I have a frozen pizza, and we can watch *Terminator*."

"Which one?"

"Two of course. That's the best one. Everyone knows that."

"It's one of the few times..." Then in unison. "...the sequel was better than the original."

Jessica knew Alex would say that because he had posted about it being one of his favorite movies and used that exact line in his post. She knew almost everything about him, including ways to get to his heart, like suggesting frozen pizza and *T2*.

They stood and quickly walked out of the restaurant like they were ditching class in high school. They bonded in that moment of defiance together. Even though they weren't breaking any rules, it still felt like they were.

01000100 01100001 01110010 01101011 00100000 01001101 01100001 01110100 01110100 01100101 01110010

Jessica managed to keep her hands on Alex the entire car ride back to her place. She held his hand for a bit before running her hand down his thigh toward his groin. Alex had never been with a woman so aggressive, and he loved every second of it. He couldn't keep his eyes off her and barely watched the road. If you asked him how they got to her house, he wouldn't have a clue. He stayed fixated on Jessica the entire ride.

It wasn't until they pulled up to a large black gate that Alex finally looked out of the car.

"Woah. This is the entrance to your house?"

She pressed a button on the roof of the car to open the gate and smiled at him.

The driveway ran through woods for more than a mile, winding all the way up to a huge house secluded from civilization. It was modern, yet comforting as you approached the house with its sparkling white siding and wood trim. Alex noticed the view of the ocean as they pulled around to the side of the house in front of the garage. The house sat on an elevated lot overlooking the Pacific, which appeared to be about a hundred feet below them. It was a spectacular view, especially with the half-moon making its way to the horizon. It was bright, one side illuminated and the dark side still hiding its face in the shadows. Alex hated heights, and looking over the cliff sent a chill up his spine and made his palms sweat.

Jessica pressed another button, and the garage opened. There were a few other cars in the garage, and it made Alex wonder if there were other people there.

"Do you have company over? Please tell me one of these cars isn't your husband's."

"No, silly! Do you see a ring on this finger?" She held up her left hand.

"Sorry." Alex blushed in embarrassment. "I didn't think you'd have this many cars. What do you do for a living?"

"I work in the healthcare industry. I do research and development. R and D they call it."

"Are you a doctor?"

She laughed. "No. I just give the doctors what they need to get their job done." Again, she rubbed her hand into his inner thigh as she rolled the car into the garage. Each time she rubbed him, his heart rate jumped, but his nerves seemed to calm all at the same time.

Alex still felt a little uneasy about going into a stranger's house. He hadn't found himself in a situation like this...ever. He had been lucky a few years back and actually got a girl to come back to his place. She wasn't impressed and never called him back. He couldn't help but think why this rich and beautiful woman would want to be with him. Most men who are down on their luck with women question the first one that comes along and actually shows them attention.

Jessica removed her hand from Alex to turn off the car. She gave him a mischievous glance and encouraged him to follow her into the house. "C'mon. Let's go."

She led him into the house and offered him something to drink. He declined alcohol because he wanted to be able to remember everything about this night. He might not get another night like this ever again in his life. Jessica pulled out a water bottle from the fridge, and while he chugged from the bottle, she stepped behind him to help take off his jacket, rubbing her hands up and down his torso. For a moment, it felt like she was scanning him like one of those TSA agents at the airport would with their wand.

Jessica lightly pinched his nipples, started giggling, and ran away from him with encouragement for him to follow. "You said you wanted to see the *Terminator*, right?"

He playfully jogged after her, and they met at the top of the stairs to the basement. He pushed his lips against hers when their bodies collided. He was over the moon. He felt like he'd do anything for this woman. This angel had fallen into his lap.

She smiled at him and started down the stairs. "Come with me if you want to live." Alex dropped his head back, laughing at her reference to the movie. Alex had been falling for Jessica the entire night, but that sent him over the edge.

The theater room in the basement looked like a

real theater, with rows of leather chairs and couches, bean bags, a popcorn machine, a bar, and a huge projection screen that took up almost the entire wall.

"Wow! This is amazing."

"You like it? It's my favorite room in the entire house."

"I mean...I don't know what to say." Alex lived for movies. He had dreamed of owning a house with a room like this. He'd never have to go to the movies and sit in front of some fat slob shoving popcorn and candy into their mouth again. Or have to listen to those annoying teenage girls gossiping during the entire movie instead of actually watching it. He could have the privacy he wanted with the authentic movie experience.

Jessica picked a couch and patted the seat to get Alex to sit with her. It was like an owner calling their dog up onto the couch to snuggle in for a movie. She pressed a button on her remote, and the screen came to life.

A video started to play.

"We don't always get second chances in life."

A woman started the advertisement, and it was one of those cliché commercials for medication that have kids running around chasing butterflies and a father and son fishing on a lake.

"With Regenerate, you now have that chance. Every organ, every blood type. We have your match and can give you an opportunity to receive your requested transplant within 24 hours."

Alex looked over at Jessica who was zoned into the TV, not making any movements or even blinking. She must really be into this commercial he thought. She is in the medical field after all.

The woman continued speaking about the various case studies, and how they had saved thousands of lives in their company's short history.

"We're changing the world one transplant at a time."

The commercial ended.

The screen remained dark, and a light came on over a door next to the screen. A woman walked out in a business suit with glasses and long blonde hair that had been straightened out flat. She had a serious look on her face as she scanned her clipboard while standing in front of the blank projector screen.

"You must be...Alex. Welcome."

Alex noticed she had the same voice as the woman from the commercial.

"Who are you? What's going on?" He turned to Jessica. "I thought you said no one else was here."

Jessica didn't move an inch and continued her zoned-out stare at the screen.

"Welcome to the Regenerate headquarters. My name's Rebecca. What did you think of our newest commercial?"

Alex hadn't freaked out yet, but he was definitely growing concerned with each second that passed. "You 3-D print organs. Seems like a huge advancement in healthcare technology. Can I go now?"

He stood from his seat looking to make an exit, but Rebecca encouraged him to stay seated. "I just have a few more questions."

"If I answer them, can I go?"

"Of course. However, I'm hoping you'll want to work here once I tell you more."

"Work here?"

"Yes, we're in need of backfilling a position, and you're a perfect candidate for the job."

"Okay..." Alex looked over at Jessica, still in the same position. "What the fuck is wrong with her? Why isn't she moving?"

"I'll explain everything. I just need to ask you a few questions before we can move on to the next step of your orientation. Can you confirm your blood type is A-positive?"

"Yeah, it is. How did you know that?"

"You donated blood to the Red Cross a few years back, and we work with them."

Learning that Regenerate worked with the American Red Cross made Alex feel a little more relaxed, but Jessica's dormant state still worried him.

"Are you a smoker?"

"I've never smoked a day in my life."

"Good. Good." Rebecca marked her clipboard a few times. "Your family history looks pretty normal. Okay, I think we're good to move on."

As soon as she finished speaking, the screen started to roll up, revealing a window. Rebecca motioned for Alex to come up to take a look. He stood and kept his eyes on Jessica, wondering why she had remained dormant this entire time. As he approached the window, he couldn't believe what he saw.

There were rows of humans lined up on metal structures for what looked like a mile long. Each person had a shaved head and tubes sticking in and out of them in several places. Their arms were spread wide, and they would have all looked like Jesus on the cross, except their legs were spread apart to form a human X. Alex scanned the area and noticed all the equipment. The facility must have cost billions of dollars to build and set up. It looked like a scene out of *The Matrix* with all the bodies lined up.

"Every time you see Reggie..."

A drone with robotic arms quickly flew across the window and zoomed away. It hovered over one of the women, and red lasers shot out from the machine like it was scanning a barcode.

"...it means a life is about to be saved. We get dozens of requests a day from all around the world for people needing organs to survive. Our tech is able to scan internal organs without invading the rep, and we 3-D print the organ to send it out to those in need. The perfect match every single time. We save dozens of lives a day, and soon we'll be able to help every single person across the globe in need of an organ to survive."

"But these are real humans you're scanning.

Are they alive?"

"Yes, but they're heavily sedated."

"How can you do that? You're holding these people hostage and stealing their organs. This is so fucked up!"

"Alex, calm down. All of them have agreed to this. They know it's for the greater good. Let me ask you this. Would you sacrifice yourself to save hundreds maybe thousands of other people?"

"I mean...yeah." For the first time, Alex realized that he could end up being one of the reps on this human farm for organs. He also thought about how the black market for organs had really changed from what he'd seen in the movies. "This is crazy. I can't do this. I want to go home. Now!"

"But you just said you want to help."

"No, I didn't. I'm not agreeing to this."

"Yes, you did." Rebecca nodded her head like she was telling someone to do something.

Suddenly, Jessica was standing right behind him, and a recording started to play. Her lips weren't moving, but the sound was definitely coming from her.

"Would you sacrifice yourself to save hundreds maybe thousands of other people?" The recording of Rebecca played, then Alex's response.

"I mean... yeah."

"I mean... yeah."

"I mean... yeah."

Alex started to feel faint. His vision swirled around, and he lost his balance, falling into one of the leather chairs. It could have been shock, but then he realized something as he reached for the water bottle Jessica gave him. He picked it up and tried to bring it into focus as his vision blurred. The medicine in the bottle worked as a time-release, weakening his muscles to avoid any chance of escape. His body felt heavy, and suddenly he couldn't move at all. This is what paralysis must feel like, he thought.

"You see, Jessica here is programmed to know everything about you. That's why it was so easy for her to connect with you. We used all the public data that you put out onto the internet to develop a report on you and your life. We need to ensure that all of our candidates fit certain criteria in order for them to be able to qualify for harvesting. We recently lost our white male with an A-positive blood type. You were a perfect match, so we dispatched one of our female androids based on your sexual preferences and had her begin communications with you through our 'dating' app. Enter Jessica."

Alex looked over at Jessica standing at attention. Everything about her seemed so real on the outside, yet everything inside so fake. He had been catfished by an android. His eyes took one final swirl, and he lost consciousness.

01000100 01100001 01110010 01101011 00100000 01001101 01100001 01110100 01110100 01100101 01110010

Beep. Beep. Beep...

The beeping sound woke Alex from his dormant state. One of the tubes connected to his body had come loose, and an alert continuously beeped to warn central command of the issue. This particular tube was responsible for keeping Alex unconscious. The tube hadn't been properly connected, and the pressure eventually pushed the tube out of place. A stream of sleeping gas shot out from the tube into the air, making a hissing sound.

It took a moment for Alex to realize where he was and what was happening. He only had a minute before Reggie would show up to check on the issue. He looked around and saw the other people surrounding him in the vast human farm for organs. He lifted one of his arms and rubbed his eyes. He was surprised his hands and legs weren't restrained, but it was unnecessary considering all the human subjects were being fed sleeping gas to keep them in a comatose state.

Alex rubbed his hands through the stubble of his newly buzzed head. He started to pull out the tubes connected to his body, one by one. Each tube released liquids and gasses to help keep him barely alive for harvest. With every tube pulled, another beeping sound started. By the time he finished removing the tubes, there was a symphony of alerts calling to central command for assistance. At this point, he had only seconds before Reggie would find him.

He tried to stand, but his legs felt like Jello. He started to slap his legs to try to get the blood flowing. He beat at them and eventually started shaking them back and forth while crippled on the ground. He felt the nerves come back into his right leg, and he figured that was all he needed to start his escape. His left leg limped behind him as he trudged along down his row past the other humans. All different races, genders, and blood types carefully mapped out and ready for harvest. Their blank faces somehow stared at him even though their eyes were closed.

Alex slowly got all the feeling back into his body and kept moving forward. That's what he told himself: "Keep moving forward. Just keep moving forward." He finally found an exit that led to a stairwell and began his ascent back to ground level. There was only one way to go anyway, and that was up.

A drone had finally come to Alex's farming location and alerted Rebecca that one of her subjects had escaped. She called on two of her male androids to search the area and find him. Not only did these droids serve as security for Rebecca, but she also used them to catfish women, or anyone with a sexual preference for men, the same way she had used Jessica on Alex. With a small army of droids at her command, she was able to create her organ farm and keep it running with little to no issue. This wasn't the first time a human had attempted an escape, and it wouldn't be the last. She sat in her office chair, staring at the photo of Alex, knowing that he would never leave her farm. A wicked smile formed on her face, but deep inside she knew what she was doing saved thousands of lives.

Alex made it to the top of the stairs and flung open the door. His naked body was hit with the morning sun as he shielded his eyes from the bright light. His breath was visible in the cold air as he panted. The door sat on the side of a shed in the backyard with the house a few hundred yards away. He turned to the woods and ran, his footprints leaving a trail in the snow.

He ran until his feet started to bleed from the branches and rocks scattered along the ground. They started to numb from the cold with each bloody imprint. His life was at stake, and he'd do whatever it took to escape.

Alex hid behind a tree and debated trying to climb up. His breath clouded the air in front of him, making it harder for him to see. His chest heaved in and out as he tried to regain his breath and slow his nerves to make the right decision. Cold, naked, and weak he knew there was only one thing to do—run.

He could hear someone behind him now, starting to gain on him, and he increased his speed out of pure adrenaline. The two male droids used their optical heat sensors to scan the area and locate Alex. They spotted him and started to run toward him like a cheetah after its prey.

Alex ran as fast as he could and felt them gaining on him. He looked back while he ran and didn't see the end of the tree line coming. Unfortunately for him, the end of the tree line was also the edge of the cliff that dropped into the Pacific. On his way down, he knew it was the end. His body hit the ocean with enough force to push his brain into his skull, instantly killing him.

The two droids made it to the edge of the cliff and looked down at Alex's floating body moving from wave to wave around the rocky shoreline. One of them scanned for any sign of life. It zeroed in on Alex's heart, and blood pumped through this critical organ for the last time. A 3-D copy of his heart would never save a life in need.

The droid finished its scan. "Subject 5732, deceased."

"I've sent the report back to Rebecca. She said leave him."

"Looks like she'll have to find another one."

The two droids turned and walked back to the farm.

01000100 01100001 01110010 01101011 00100000 01001101 01100001 01110100 01110100 01100101 01110010

He sat at the bar rocking his leg up and down in anticipation. He didn't get nervous, but this felt different. Maybe it was because he never really did the online dating thing. He was good with women in person. He hated texting. He'd rather meet a girl at a bar or a grocery store. He could use his slick syntax to sway almost any girl into his arms. But this wasn't any girl. This was the *perfect* girl.

He downed the last sip of his drink and motioned to the bartender for another. He needed the liquid courage to calm his nerves. His eyes fixated on the door every five seconds waiting for her to walk through. Finally, she did. Even though he had seen her picture online, it was love at first sight.

She looked the same as before, except for one detail. Her hair was now red. That was his preference. She slowly walked toward him, and he eyed her up with his mouth agape. She was his dream girl, and for once he couldn't speak. Yeah, he had good looks, but his bread and butter was how he could swoon a woman with his words.

Finally, she broke the silence. "You must be Noah."

"And you must be Jessica."

SWARM

Swarm

We never know what's beneath the surface. We all have our secrets, and I finally brought mine to light. I was sick of living a lie and letting it run my life. No, *ruin* my life. Now that it's out in the open, there's a huge weight off my shoulders. I still feel like crap for cheating on him, but at least Ben and I are being honest with each other now. I made one mistake, and I'll never make it again. Especially now that Ben has forgiven me. I wouldn't know what to do if I lost our family. That's my number one goal right now—keeping our family together.

It seems a little too quiet in the car, so I glance at the backseat. Our oldest, Tommy, is asleep with his head against the window and drool sliding down the corner of his mouth. I can't believe he's going to college in a few years. My daughter, Julie, is zoned in on her tablet with her headphones covering her ears. As a preteen, it's rare to see her without her headphones on blocking out the rest of the world. I've never been so thankful to have my family together as we start a new chapter of our lives, but a part of me still hates myself for what I did to Ben.

"Kate?" He grabs my attention out of my daze.

"Yeah?"

"I know what you're thinking, and you need to stop."

"How do you know what I'm thinking?"

"We've been married for 18 years." He rubs my hand gently. "You can't beat yourself up about it anymore. It's over. It's time to move on. That's what this house is all about, right?"

"Yeah, you're right."

A few minutes later we turn into the driveway of our new vacation home on the river. It's only a few hours away from D.C. and gives us a chance to break away from the hamster wheel for a few days. It's our first trip to the house since we bought it, and I can't wait to start decorating. We have furniture being delivered tomorrow, and making this vacation house a home is my priority for the long weekend.

"Woah! Is that the new house?" Julie yells out since her noise-canceling headphones block her ability to hear how loud she's talking.

Startled from his nap, Tommy yells out, "What the fuck, Julie?!"

"Hey, watch your mouth!" Ben gives a death

stare to Tommy through the rearview mirror.

"Alright, everyone. Calm down." I seem to always be the voice of reason in the family. "Can we please try to be nice to each other for our first visit to the new house?"

Tommy rolls his eyes at me when I look to the backseat. "Who buys a summer house at the *end* of summer anyway?"

"Just because it's a summer house, doesn't mean we can't use it all year. It'll be a nice place to get away from time to time. Don't you think?"

Tommy huffs his teenage, post-nap pout at me.

"I think the house looks B-E-A-You-Tifull!" Julie says at a normal volume now that her headphones are off.

The front yard has nice landscaping, but it could use some work. The driveway wraps around to the front of the house in a U-shape with a small patch of bushes and plants in the middle of the yard.

"Let's go check it out." Ben turns off the ignition after parking in the driveway, and we all exit the car.

The brick house sits on top of a hill that leads down to the river. You can see the water looking down the side of the house, and Julie catches a glimpse. "C'mon!" She runs toward the dock, encouraging us to follow her.

Standing in the backyard at the top of the hill looking down on the glassy river with our arms around each other, I finally feel like we have our family back in one piece. Everyone seems happy. Even Tommy has put away his teenage angst and has a smile on his face. I look around and don't see another house or sign of life for miles. The seclusion of this house sealed the deal for us since we wanted to find something off the grid. Our own little hideaway where nothing can bother us. I can feel my smile stretching to my ears as the kids dip their toes in the water to gauge its temperature.

Suddenly, a bug flies right past my ear and makes me jump out of Ben's arms. "What in the world was that?"

"I think it was a horsefly or a bee." Ben softly rubs my back. "You okay?"

"Yeah, it just scared me is all." I swallow the mucus that's built up in my mouth. "I don't think that was a bee. It looked like a wasp."

"It's gone, honey. Let's just enjoy this moment. This beautiful view. Our beautiful children. A new house on the river. A fresh start ... for us." Ben leans in and kisses me.

"Get a room!" Tommy yells back at us.

We unpack the car and get settled in the house. I make an easy pasta dinner with Julie while the boys move boxes. We lay out blankets and pillows and watch a movie with our TV sitting on the floor leaning up against the wall. The kids fall asleep watching the movie, and Ben and I head to our room.

I'm lying on our new mattress on the floor next to Ben anxious with all the excitement and the unsettling feeling that comes with sleeping in a new house for the first time. I can't wait for our furniture delivery tomorrow to start putting things in place. There's something else I can't get out of my mind—the sound of the wasp buzzing by my ear.

01000100 01100001 01110010 01101011 00100000 01001101 01100001 01110100 01110100 01100101 01110010

The best way to wake a house up in the morning is with the smell of bacon. It seems to always do the trick when I want to get the family up and at 'em. I've been up since five with my mind continuing to race with all the things I want to do for the day. I've already picked up paint supplies from the store this morning. The furniture delivery is supposed to arrive between three and five this afternoon, which gives me plenty of time to paint some of the walls and start working on the house. The kids are going to help me paint, and Ben wants to work on the yard.

"Mommy? Where's my tablet?"

"It's in the car, Julie. No tablets today."

"Ugh fine. Can we go in the water after breakfast? I can't wait to jump off the dock!" Julie's eagerness is spewing out of her. At eleven years old, she wears her emotions on her sleeve. She's going to be a handful when she's a teenager.

"We have a lot to do today, sweetie. I want to get the painting done before the furniture gets here. I thought you guys were gonna help me."

I sweep a pile of scrambled eggs onto the kids' plates.

"So, our first day at the river and we can't even go in the water? What is this? Nazi Germany?" Tommy loves to laugh at his own jokes.

I smile at him knowing my anxiousness is taking over when I should be using this time to connect with the family. "You're right. After breakfast, we can go in the water for a little bit."

"Yeah!" Julie screams out with eggs in her mouth.

"I'm going to get started on the yard early." Ben's looking down at his phone. "I don't want to be out working in the sun later today. It's supposed to get up into the high 90s."

It would be nice for him to stay with the family, but I understand why he wants to get an outdoor project like that done before it gets too hot.

The plate of bacon in the middle of the table is almost gone after everyone piles their plate up with the delicious meat. Ben takes a call at the table. I can tell it's a work call based on the cadence of his speech when he answers. He gets up from the table and heads into our bedroom, and I think about how his addiction to work was one of the reasons I ended up cheating on him. All those late nights working and the attention given to his work that was never spent on me. I hate that the thought creeps into my head, but I had hoped this would be a place devoid of work and an opportunity for us to focus on our family. Now, he's getting up during our first damn breakfast together.

I take a deep breath and convince myself his dedication to his work is the reason we can even afford this vacation house. His work ethic is one of the things that initially attracted me to Ben, but it also turned out to be the reason I cheated on him. We're both working on being supportive in these situations. I make a mental note to talk to him about it later, though. I'm hoping he can find a way to unplug and focus on the family.

"Go get your bathing suits on, kids." I figure I can use a little relaxation and read my book by the water while the kids play.

I head into the bedroom to change while Ben's on the phone. Instead of berating him about skipping out on our family breakfast, I take a different approach. Standing at the closed door right in his line of sight as he lies on the bed, I drop my shorts to the ground. My theatrical production continues as I grab my shirt with both hands and slowly pull it over my head so I'm only in my underwear. I turn around for him to see my backside as I pull my underwear up to accentuate my curves to him. He talks into the phone almost in slow motion asking the person on the other line to hold on for a second. I take my underwear down to my ankles bending over invitingly. Now fully naked, I strut into the bathroom curling my pointer finger in and out inviting him to join me.

"Sorry. I gotta go." He leaves his phone on the

bed and follows me into the bathroom like a puppy. He grabs me by the waist spinning me around and pushes me against the wall. His lips press against mine, and I can feel him getting excited as he presses himself up against my leg.

Knock. Knock. Knock.

"Mommy!" Julie yells through the door. "Can we go down to the water now?"

"In a minute, honey!" My breathing accelerates while Ben kisses my neck.

"But I can't find my bathing suit!"

"Alright ... I'll be right there." Peeling away from Ben, I offer him a rain check. "Wait for the kids to go to bed tonight?"

"It's a date."

I put on my bathing suit and grab my book to read by the water. Ben gets dressed and heads outside through the garage with a sly grin on his face knowing what he's in store for later. I open the front door and look through the glass on the storm door as he puts on his gloves. Standing there with his muscles stretching the short sleeves of his shirt, I wish I had never cheated on him. He's a great husband and drop-dead gorgeous. It feels like I'm falling in love with him all over again, and I couldn't be happier.

01000100 01100001 01110010 01101011 00100000 01001101 01100001 01110100 01110100 01100101 01110010

When Ben suggested living in a house on the river, I thought he was joking. Looking out at this view from the dock, it's quickly growing on me. Seeing Julie and Tommy jumping off the dock and playing around in the water with those huge smiles on their faces puts one on mine. It seems as though I can't stop smiling today.

A jet ski zooms by a few hundred yards out from us. The buzzing of the engine catches Tommy's ear, and he turns back to me sitting on the dock. "We gotta get one of those, Mom!"

I chuckle and give him a look that says, "Maybe." We've already dropped more than half of our savings for the down payment on the house. We certainly can afford it, but I'm not sure we're in a position to start buying toys, especially with the money we're spending on furnishing the house. And who knows what kind of repairs or fixes this place might need.

I've only been sitting here for a few minutes, and I'm already in love with our new paradise. My sister and her family are going to love this place. I take a picture of the kids in the water with the view in the background and send it to her with a message—"Loving the new place! Can't wait for you to visit!!"

I set the phone down on the dock. Right when I open my book to its marked page, a scream echoes from the direction of the house. *That couldn't have been Ben.*

Again, another scream. And this one is loud. It's one of those screams you never want to hear in your lifetime. A scream that can haunt you forever.

The kids look up at me with confused faces wondering what's going on. *It's definitely, Ben.*

I throw my book down, leap from my chair, and run up the hill toward the house. The kids instinctively follow me, and a loud hum hits my eardrums. A buzzing. But not like the jet ski. It's the same noise I heard last night when that wasp flew by my ear but times a thousand. Then, another horrific scream. It sounds like someone's murdering my husband. I run around the house with both kids at my side and put my hands out to stop them as soon as I see why Ben keeps screaming.

A large swarm of black and yellow wasps are covering his upper body and head as he crawls on all fours toward the house. I can see more wasps coming up from underneath the ground in the center of the yard under some brush behind him. I can barely see Ben's face with so many of the wasps wrapped around his head. He starts to scream in loud, high-pitched intervals of a few seconds. "Ahh! ... Ahh! ... AHH! ... AHH! ..."

"Ben!" I yell out to him to get his attention, but I'm not sure he'll even be able to hear me over the wasps and his own screaming.

"Daddy!" Julie yells out, and the pitch of her voice catches his attention.

Ben manages to lift one of his arms and wave it toward the house. "Get ... inside!" His voice is muffled behind the swarm and the sound of the wasps. A few of them zoom around me and the kids, and I pull them into the garage through the side door of the house. Something clicks in me, and I realize I should make sure the house is locked up. No windows or doors open so they can get in. I'm following Ben's lead and need to make sure the kids are safe.

After quickly checking for any openings, I run to the storm door in the front of the house. Ben's now lying on his back almost completely covered in wasps. There are thousands of them crawling all over him and flying around his body. He's not moving, and at this point, I'm not even sure if he's alive. His stomach pumps up and down in quick, shallow breaths and then stops moving.

I *need* to get to him. I *need* to save him. But then it sinks in. I *can't* save him. If I try, I'll be putting myself and the kids in danger. Still, I feel like I owe it to Ben after everything that's happened. I almost wish it was me out there and not him. I'm the one who almost tore our family apart.

What makes it even worse is there are still more wasps coming out of the ground.

I crash to my knees, and Julie climbs into my arms crying her eyes out.

Tommy's standing in shock as his wide eyes stay focused on his dad.

I have absolutely no idea what to do. I try to compose myself by taking a deep breath.

Clink. Clink ... Clink. Clink. Clink.

The wasps start hitting the translucent storm

door. I look closely, and they aren't running into it by accident like a bird flying into a window they don't see. The wasps are *attacking* the door.

"I'm going to get him." Tommy grabs the handle of the front door.

"Like hell you are!" I grab Tommy's arm before he can make a move outside. "It's too dangerous."

"Dad wouldn't leave one of us out there to die. We *have* to do something!"

"You heard him, Tommy. He told us to get inside. There's too many of them, and I'm not putting you in any more danger."

Tommy focuses his attention on the door handle as if still debating whether to go outside.

"Please, Tommy. Don't do it."

His shoulders sink in defeat, and he stands back from the door. I let out a long breath in relief knowing there's nothing Tommy can do to save his dad right now.

The wasps continue to pound on the glass door. Focusing on one of the wasps, it's about as long as my pinky finger and it looks angry. I'm not sure how you can tell if something is angry even when it doesn't really have a face, but I can somehow tell. It's pushing its stinger forward when it hits the glass. It stays connected, and it's almost as if it's staring right at me saying, "We're coming for you, too. You mess with our house, we're going to mess with yours,"—assuming Ben ruffled their nest. Wasps don't just attack for no reason.

I can't believe I haven't called 9-1-1 yet! Maybe

they can get here in time and save him.

Julie's clinging to me for dear life, and I peel her off my body. "Tommy. Take your sister. Where's my fucking phone?!" I scramble around the house looking for it, but I can't find it. Then it hits me.

My phone is at the dock. Shit!

"Tommy, where's your phone?"

He's still standing at the door blankly staring out at his limp father with his arm around Julie. Both create a puddle of river water beneath them as their bathing suits drip onto the floor.

"Tommy?! Where. Is. Your. Phone?" I stretch the words out so he can understand me in his state of shock.

He pats the pockets of his swim trunks. Nothing. "I took it out of my pocket to get in the water." I can see his face come to a realization and then disappointment settles in. "It's on the dock."

I look out the back window and a few dozen wasps are flying around. They're starting to bang against the glass, but it's not nearly as many as in the front yard. I run through the options in my head.

Can I use Ben's laptop to send for help?

Is there another way to get a call out to 911?

If I get stung, will I end up like Ben?

Is he dead already?

Do I want to leave the kids in the house alone by themselves?

Do I take the chance and run down to grab one of the phones real quick?

Maybe there's something I can get to help ward off any wasps when I make a run for it.

That seems to be my only option. I don't know the password to Ben's laptop, Julie left her tablet in the car, and there's no landline in the house. We have no way of communicating with the outside world unless I run to the car or can get to that dock. There are fewer wasps in the back, so the dock seems like the best option at this point.

I run to the hallway closet where some cleaning supplies were left by the previous tenants.

"Ahha!" I grab a can of wasp repellent sitting behind a big bottle of bleach and run to the front door. Tommy's still staring blankly, and Julie's crying while holding on to him for dear life. I pull Tommy by the shoulder to turn him around. "Sweetie. I need your help."

He stares back at me like he's trying to put everything together and figure out if this is a dream, real life, or a nightmare.

"I need you to open and close the back door for me. I'm going to make a run for it and try to get one of the phones." I shake his shoulder. "Tommy!? Can you do that for me? Dad needs us right now."

He shakes his head, and I can see him start to come out of his trance. "Yeah ... yeah, I can do that, Mom."

All three of us head for the back door.

"Mommy, no!" Julie yells at me and clutches my leg. It reminds me of when she used to do this as a toddler. She'd latch onto my leg and sit on my foot while I trudged around the house like Frankenstein's monster.

I bend down and grab her by the arm. "Baby, please. I have to do this, or Daddy won't have a chance. I need you to be strong for me. You're a strong, brave, young woman. Let's do this for Daddy. Whaddya say?" I run the outside of my pointer finger down her cheek wiping her tears away.

She doesn't respond but nods her head in agreement.

"Okay. Here's the plan." I have both kids kneeling in front of me so we're all eye to eye. "Tommy's going to open the door, and I'm going to run out quickly so you can shut it before any wasps can get into the house. This is so important, Tommy. You have to shut the door as soon as I cross the threshold."

He nods his head in agreement. "Got it."

"Julie. You stay behind your brother so he can protect you. If any wasps come in, make sure you shut the door *before* you try to attack them. There's a magazine in the bathroom you can use. Julie, go run and grab it."

She nods her head and runs to get the magazine.

I turn to Tommy. "Do whatever you can to save her. Don't let any wasps in and *do not* open the door for any other reason except to let me in. If the wasps are swarming me like they did your father ..." I take a big gulp of saliva and my mouth is instantly dry. "Don't let me back in the house."

"Mom ... no. I can't do that."

"It won't be safe! You'll put Julie and yourself in danger of being attacked, too. Promise me."

He nods his head in approval.

"Promise me!"

"Okay, okay. I promise."

I look out of the glass on the back door. More wasps are making their way to the back of the house, and some are even crawling on the door. I'm running out of time. The dock is about fifty yards away, and I'm worried about going up and down the hill with the potential of being attacked by these murderous monsters. I give Tommy one more command. "Make sure you don't swing the door open too hard or the wasps clinging to the door will get into the house."

Julie comes back with the magazine and hands it to Tommy while she wipes the last few tears from her cheeks.

"Alright. You guys ready?"

Tommy puts his hand on the door handle and guides Julie with his other arm to get her to stand behind him.

"On three. One ... two ... three!"

Tommy swings the door open slowly but still with a quickness to it. I run outside with the wasp-repellent can in my hand. The buzzing from the wasps fills the air so much I can hear the larger swarm in front of the house from back here. I get about ten yards out and can feel them zoning in on me as more and more wasps start to buzz around. There are so many I stop running and decide to start using the repellent. The cap to the spray is still on, and I can't believe I forgot to take it off while I was in the house. I fumble trying to get it open with the thought of being stung at any moment increases my heart rate with every beat. I finally manage the cap and start spraying the white liquid stream out of the container hitting several wasps as they start to scatter. There's a pinch on my forearm.

A pain I've never felt before runs through my whole body like an electric shock. The sting feels like electricity is streaming through my body as I see blue and white sparks, and my vision goes blurry for a moment. I manage to keep spraying, but I don't think it's doing anything. The pain from the sting is enormous, and I scream out like Ben did only a few minutes ago.

Muffled screams from the kids break me out of the initial shock.

I feel disoriented and have trouble figuring out which direction the dock is and if I can even still make it. My vision finally focuses, and the house is in front of me after spinning around a few times. I'm being attacked and decide to ditch the plan.

I'm running back and Tommy swings the door open for me. I jump through the opening and land on my side with a heavy thump. I look down at my arm and see the wasp that stung me attached to my arm trying to pull itself out or continue to dig its way into my skin with its venom. I can't tell which, and I smack it dead with my hand. Apparently, wasps don't die when they sting you. They can just keep stinging you over and over again.

A few other wasps get into the house, and Tommy smashes one against a window with the magazine. Julie screams as one of the wasps flies right by her head. Tommy pushes her out of the way and waves the magazine at the invading insect. After a few swings, he manages to kill another one. All three of us look around for more, but it looks like there aren't any more left to strike down.

My arm is throbbing as the venom takes hold in my bloodstream. The swelling is already starting to puff out, and this is only one sting. I can't imagine what it would feel like to be stung multiple times like Ben. I instinctively run to the front door to check on him. I'm not sure if I scream out in pain from the sting or the fact that my husband is most likely dead.

Ben is completely covered in wasps to the point I can only see the tips of his shoes poking out of the mass of wasps overtaking his body. They're crawling into his mouth as no part of him is off limits. Both kids attach themselves to me and start crying. Tears flow from my eyes, and I start banging at the glass trying to hit the wasps clinging to the door.

"Go away! Get the fuck away from my family!"

I continue to beat on the door and instead of scaring the wasps away, it only attracts more of them to the house.

"You damned wasps! Fuck you!"

"Mom. Mom. Stop." Tommy pulls me away from the door and hugs me while I cry into his shoulder. Julie wraps her arms around both of us as we mourn the loss of their father.

01000100 01100001 01110010 01101011 00100000 01001101 01100001 01110100 01110100 01100101 01110010

This is unbelievable, and not in a "wow this is amazing" type of way. I can't wrap my head around how this is even a thing. There are thousands of wasps outside of our house and more are still pouring out of the nest in the ground. A news story I saw a while back clicks into my brain.

A man was doing yard work and suffered multiple wasp stings. He was taken to the hospital and died shortly after. From what I remember, he was stung at least a hundred times. It also stated there were an estimated 2,500 wasps in the nest from that incident. I didn't think that was possible until I saw that news story. Based on that information, I'd say this nest has well over five thousand—maybe even closer to ten thousand.

"You alright, Mom?" Tommy holds my arm in his hands examining the sting now swelling up to look like half of a pink tennis ball.

I wince in pain as a small shock pinches my arm. The intense urge to want to scratch the sting area is strong, but I hold back. I yell out again as the pain from the sting intensifies.

"Come with me." Tommy pulls at my other arm, and we run to my bathroom. He runs the water in the sink and tells me to clean the sting area with soap and water. I'm cleaning the sting gently and clenching my teeth hard when Tommy comes back into the room with baking soda and a few medical supplies. He dries my arm with a clean towel and starts mixing some baking soda in a cup of water. He stirs it around with a spoon and looks at it with approval.

"Okay. Hold still." His voice is calm and focused.

I hold my arm steady with my opposite hand. He applies the baking soda solution, covers it with gauze, and wraps it with a bandage. I feel instant relief and the urge to scratch the sting goes away.

"The baking soda counteracts the venom from the sting."

"How do you know all this, Tommy?"

"Remember when I told you and Dad that I wanted to be a doctor? Well, I was serious about it. Plus, I read up on how to treat stings a few weeks ago when my friend got stung by a bee."

Well, I'll be damned, I think to myself and wonder how my little boy grew up so fast.

"Where's your sister?"

As soon as the words escape my mouth, we hear Julie scream from the other room. We both run out of the bathroom and find her on the floor under a blanket with a wasp buzzing around her. As we approach, I grab a small throw pillow and Tommy grabs the magazine from earlier.

"Stay there, Julie." My voice is calm and collected. "Don't. Move."

I find myself in a good position to take a swing at the hovering wasp. I look over at Tommy, and he nods his head in approval. I try to reduce any kind of backswing and quickly jerk the pillow forward at the wasp and miss. It buzzes around and then it's gone.

"Did you get it?" Tommy asks nervously as he looks around the room for it.

"No. I missed."

Julie peeks her head out of the blanket. "Is it gone?"

I wait a moment to listen for any buzzing and don't hear anything. Somehow the silence is riddled with more anxiety than the actual buzzing would be.

"I think it's gone," I tell her, fully knowing we

now have a wasp roaming around the house somewhere along with the thousands of other wasps lurking outside waiting for their moment to strike.

"We need better weapons." I'm talking to myself out loud, but the kids hear me and understand the assignment. A magazine and a pillow aren't going to do much if more of these little assholes get into the house. I get to the garage door hoping to find some good options in there and pause before opening the door.

Did I close the garage door leading out into the yard?

I can't remember and stand frozen with my hand on the door.

"Mom? What's wrong?"

"Do you remember if I closed the side door when we came in before?"

"I don't ..." he pinches his chin as if it will help him remember better. "Yeah. I think you did."

"This isn't an *I think* scenario. This is life or death! Do you know for sure if I closed it?"

"Yes. You closed it. I remember hearing the sound of it shutting."

I put my ear close to the door to listen for the buzzing sound of the wasps potentially in the garage. Nothing. I can only hear the hum of the swarm consistently coming from outside the house.

"Stay here."

"Mom, no." Tommy grabs my shoulder.

"This is a solo mission." I feel the sting in my arm pulse and suddenly have the urge to itch it. My vision is gone for a split second—either from the venom running through my veins or from the stress of our situation. I'm not sure. Maybe both. All I know is I don't want to put my kids in any more danger.

"No, it's not. Let me come with you." He pulls the magazine out of his back pocket. "I can swat any wasps that might be in there while you look for more weapons. You're always saying we're a team, right?"

I weigh the cons of this option and have to agree with Tommy. Having him in there protecting me while I search for another weapon is a good plan.

I nod in agreement. "Alright. Just like before. On three. One ... two ... three."

We enter the mugginess of the garage, and I instantly check to see if the door is closed. A deep relief overcomes me when I see it's shut. I run over to the door and twist the lock on the door thinking that will somehow keep them away.

Damnit! Why couldn't we have parked the car inside the garage instead of the driveway?!

I look around for a new weapon, and Tommy keeps his eyes moving above our heads in search of any rogue wasps. I'm rifling through a few boxes we brought in last night but don't find anything useful. The familiar buzzing sound haunting me for the past twenty-four hours enters my ears. It sounds like a mini-helicopter is hovering over us, and the enemy is approaching for the kill.

Tommy waves the magazine in the air. "Got 'em!"

"Hey, you're getting pretty good at that."

A sinister grin paints the canvas of his face. Revenge can feel good sometimes I guess.

"Ahha!" I run over to the corner of the garage and find an old tennis racket. "This should do the trick."

"Wish there was more than one."

"I dunno. That rolled-up magazine seems to be working just fine for you."

Tommy continues to scan the air for more rogue wasps.

I suddenly realize Julie's inside the house by herself and quickly run to her. I have to remember there's still a wasp inside the house that we didn't get yet. I'm hoping it hasn't zeroed in on Julie. When I swing the door open, she's on the floor with her knees pulled up to her chest and tears streaming down her face.

"You left me alone!" A bellowing sob jumps from her mouth as she sucks her bottom lip in and out with each rapid breath she takes. "Please don't leave me alone again!"

"I'm so sorry, sweetie." I pull her into my arms.

"I heard the buzzing again."

Tommy looks around the hallway with his magazine cocked in his hand.

I lift my ears a bit to see if I can hear anything

as we silently stalk the flying insect. The only thing I can hear is Julie sniffling and the heavy hum coming from the swarm outside the house. I motion Tommy to sit on the floor, and both of us wrap Julie in our arms.

"I won't leave you again, Julie. I promise." It's sweet to hear Tommy consoling Julie. He's usually the one taunting her, but this time he's her protector.

"Stay with her," I whisper to Tommy as I stand to head to the front door. Not sure why I thought there might be any change, but Ben is still lying on the grass toes up covered in wasps. I'm not sure if you can feel it when you're in shock, but looking out at Ben and examining our situation makes me realize the shock has passed, and pure panic has taken over. My chest heaves in and out with each breath as I try to calm myself down. *Is this really how Ben dies? Is this really how all of us are going to die?* I'm not the religious type, but I close my eyes and pray for us to make it out alive with a sliver of hope Ben can still make it.

By this time, there aren't as many wasps coming out of the nest in the ground but they're *still* coming nonetheless. *How many damned wasps are in this nest?*

I walk around the house and see thousands of them either flying around aggressively or walking on the windows. The loud buzzing from the swarm almost vibrates my body and melds to my brain like a hypnotic hum or a song you can't get out of your head. I also hear a scratching noise as I'm looking through a sea of wasps on a closed window in one of the bedrooms. It sounds like their legs are walking on the screen as I focus on one of the wasps. Then I hear a click like a latch falling open. I run to the sound coming from the kitchen area and have my tennis racket in hand.

The good news is one of the windows in the kitchen was left open but thankfully it has a screen. The bad news is there are hundreds of wasps pushing up against the screen, and it's starting to give way.

"Tommy!" I yell out in a high-pitched screech. "Get the wasp spray!"

I have seconds before these wasps finish pushing through this screen window and the entire swarm will have free reign of our new house. Several of them creep through the side of the screen, and they start to buzz around the kitchen frantically. I slam the window shut as more wasps try to make their entrance.

One of the wasps hovers over my already bitten arm like it's attracted to the venom lingering under my skin. I quickly step back to swing the racket and make contact.

Tommy rushes into the kitchen with the wasp spray in one hand and Julie's hand in the other. I raise my hands as if to let him know I'm ready to catch the spray. As I catch the can and look up, several wasps continue flying around the kitchen.

"Get out of here! Get Julie and go to my room!"

Tommy hesitates, wondering if he should help me, but nods his head and quickly leads Julie to the bedroom.

As soon as I hear the door shut, a wasp lands on my leg and a shock ripples through my body to my head causing my vision to blur. A grunting scream escapes my mouth echoing against the walls of the kitchen. The pain intensifies, and I drop the racket to free my hand to slap the wasp dead. My focus quickly turns to getting rid of the other wasps buzzing around the kitchen despite being stung for the second time.

I know you're not supposed to spray these cans inside the house, but I'm not looking to get bit by one of these things a third time. The white liquid comes flying out of the can like Spider-Man's webs as I press the spray button. It catches one of the wasps, and it lands on the floor. I finish it off with another spray for good measure. The other wasps scatter, and I try to track them one by one. I pick up the racket and make contact with a couple of them as I swing frantically. With the can in my left and the racket in my right, I'm becoming pretty deadly.

There are only a few remaining wasps, but they fly out of the kitchen and head to the other side of the house—thankfully away from the bedroom. The kids seem safe when I get to the bedroom and slam the door shut before running to the closet to get a towel. I shove it in the bottom of the door and make sure it's tight against the edges so none of them can squeeze through. Again, for some reason, I think locking the door will add an extra layer of protection.

After applying more of the baking soda solution to my leg, Tommy lies on the bed with his arms around Julie cuddled up in a ball. I join them and whisper in their ears, "It's okay. It's going to be okay." As the words escape my mouth, I wonder how true they actually are. Part of me doesn't think we'll get out of here alive and that we'll all end up like Ben. Unless I do something about it. But what?

The best thing I can do right now is squeeze my children while the buzzing from the swarm vibrates our house.

01000100 01100001 01110010 01101011 00100000 01001101 01100001 01110100 01110100 01100101 01110010

Several hours pass as the adrenaline from the first wave of attacks wears off. The venom from the stings is making me drowsy, and I'm struggling to keep my eyes open. We've been safe in my room for a while now as the hot summer sun tries to shine through the wasps clinging to the outside of our house. Rays of light make their way through the dense swarm, but it still feels like a dark cloud is holding our world hostage from the sunlight.

I'm sitting in a chair next to the mattress where Ben and I slept together only a few hours ago—the last time we will ever sleep together. I feel the urge to scratch the sting on my leg under the new bandage Tommy applied. I'm watching both kids like a hawk with my eye on the door to make sure any intruding insects don't sneak their way inside. I need to do whatever it takes to protect my kids.

A ray of sunlight makes its way through and hits Julie in the face waking her up from her catnap. "I'm hungry."

Tommy wakes up and stretches out. "Me too."

It's almost three o'clock. The delivery truck should be here any minute with our furniture. That might be our chance to get someone from the outside to call 9-1-1.

I sit up and head to my purse sitting by the door. I keep my eyes on the towel and check for any openings while I rummage through my purse.

"Here you go." Luckily, I have two protein bars and give them to the kids. My stomach can't take any food right now. The only thing I'm focused on is saving our family. A tear falls off my face and hits the top of my hand. Poor Ben. My poor, sweet husband. The grief starts to overtake me, and I can't stop the flood of tears streaming from my eyes.

"What's wrong, Mommy?" Julie's mouth is full of food.

"Nothing, sweetie. Nothing." I wipe the final tears away and hug her. "The delivery truck should be here soon. They're supposed to come between three and five. We need to have a plan for when they get here."

Tommy takes a bite of his bar. "They're either

going to get attacked by the swarm, or they'll see it and drive away."

"Not unless we can somehow get their attention."

"Mom ... we can't open any doors, and now the windows aren't even safe to open."

I push my face into my palms trying to find the best plan. Luckily, the bedroom is on the corner of the house and has windows facing the river and the driveway.

"We'll just have to bang on the glass when they pull up and try to get their attention." All of us sit in silence (except for the humming from the swarm in the background) trying to figure out what to do. "I got it!"

A black Sharpie sits at the bottom of my purse ready to save the day. I run to the closet in the bathroom to look for a bed sheet but don't find one. There's a roll of duct tape that fits nicely in with my plan. "Off the bed. Off the bed. Quick!" I frantically pull the sheets off the bed as the kids climb off.

"What are you doing, Mommy?" Julie grabs onto Tommy.

"We don't have much time. They could be here any minute. Help me lay the sheet out."

All three of us pull the bed sheet wide so it's lying flat on the ground. I pull the cap off the marker and start writing. The result is a white sheet with "WASPS! S.O.S." written in all caps in black marker. Tommy helps me spread the sheet across one half of the window, and we use the duct tape to keep it up against the window displaying our call for help but also leaving the other half of the window for us to try to wave them down. *This is going to work.*

"Tommy. Stand by the window and call out if you see the truck pull up."

Julie grabs my hand, and I lead her onto the bed.

"You alright?"

"I'm okay. Is Daddy going to be okay?"

"I dunno, sweetie." I look over at Tommy, and we connect eyes. He looks back out into the front yard, and I know he's looking at his father's dead body lying in the grass because anger grows on his face. He wants revenge, and so do I.

I put my arm around Julie and keep her close. I glance at my watch—ten past three—and hope the delivery truck will be here closer to the beginning of their delivery window and not the end. I start to sing "You Are My Sunshine" to try to calm Julie, but really it's helping calm me down, too.

After the first verse, Tommy screams, "They're here!"

Julie and I run to the window, and all three of us are waving our hands frantically and yelling out for help.

A big white box truck pulls into the driveway slowly and stops about halfway down parallel to where Ben's body is lying on the ground. I'm hoping they can see our makeshift sign in the window through the fog of wasps clinging to the window and put two and two together.

Tommy starts banging on the window, and the wasps scatter off the screen. It seems to draw more wasps but also gets them away from the window to hopefully allow one of the delivery guys to see our S.O.S. sign more clearly.

The man in the passenger seat slowly exits the truck with a confused look on his face. He's squinting his eyes and staring right into the window at us. The driver gets out of the truck and starts walking toward Ben. I can see his lips moving and assume he's trying to communicate with my dead husband. *Get back in the truck and call 9-1-1!*

Some of the wasps are already gravitating toward them and some of them are flying around their truck, which now has both of its doors open. Time is slowly fading away for them to be able to save us. The passenger starts walking toward us with his hands out to the side as if to say, *"What in the hell is going on here?"* Then he slaps his hand on his arm. He's been stung. The cloud of wasps around him starts to darken, and they go in for the kill pecking at his face, neck, arms, legs, and pretty much any open skin. His screams pierce the air as he crumbles to his knees. I know how he feels as the pain in my arm and leg from my stings pulsates.

The gravity of the situation clicks for the driver as he sees Ben's lifeless body covered in wasps from close up and then his partner screaming in agony. He turns to run toward the truck and sees the wasps buzzing inside the cabin. Panic sets in as he turns toward the house and sees our sign for the first time. A look of pure terror overtakes his face as his eyes widen and his chin drops. He runs around the truck to find his friend curled up on his side with muffled screams through the clump of wasps covering his mouth.

"They're not gonna make it," Tommy says in a way too calm voice.

"The driver still has a chance!" I continue banging on the window, and the kids follow my lead as we yell out trying to get his attention and point toward the front door.

He stumbles back away from the passenger and falls on his backside. He hears our calls, and I make eye contact with him. I point toward the front door as if to say, "*Get to the door and I'll let you inside.*"

By waving him to the front door, I now have to go back out into the rest of the house where there could be more wasps waiting. This may be our only chance of getting out of here alive, so I have to take the risk.

"Stay here with your sister and put the towel back when I close the door."

Tommy nods at me with a calming look in his eyes. I take a moment to cherish how unbelievably brave he's been during this situation.

I quickly exit the room and shut the door

behind me pausing to listen. There's buzzing coming from inside the house. I'm creeping down the hallway with my eyes tracking for wasps high and low. As I approach the entrance to the kitchen, I can hear the buzzing getting louder. *Damnit! Didn't I shut the window in there? How the fuck are they getting into the house!?*

I inch my way to the entryway of the kitchen and peek my head around the frame. As soon as I see the dozens of wasps in the kitchen, I pull my head back and lean against the wall with my hand cupped to my mouth to avoid making any loud noises or gasps. The last thing I want is for them to hear me—honestly, I'm not sure if they are even attracted to sounds, but I'm not taking that chance.

I'm holding my breath as I slide past the entryway and escape without them noticing me. Luckily, they're all hanging around the kitchen, and none of them follow me to the front door. I look through the storm door and see the delivery driver crawling toward the steps in an attempt to get to the door while he's screaming in agony. He has hundreds of wasps crawling all over him. His face is already swollen from what I can see. I focus in on a wasp stinging him on the side of his neck repeatedly. He's too far away from the door for me to pull him in, and there's no way I'm saving him now. *These things are vicious.*

He finally crumbles to the ground and gives up when he reaches the first step to our porch. More wasps cling to the storm door, and one of them sneaks through a small crack in the bottom of the storm door that doesn't quite sit flush with the frame. One more crawls through, then another. I slam the main door shut and run to the bedroom as fast as I can.

As I'm cramming the towel into the bottom of the bedroom door, I realize—if these things can crawl through tiny cracks like they did in the kitchen window and front door, I'm not sure how long this towel will hold them out of our room.

The kids are standing at the window watching their father and the two delivery guys being ravaged by the wasps. I stand by the window next to them, watching in shock. Hope for any chance of survival feels minimal at this point. I need to protect my children. *How can I save them?* That's all I care about, and it's the only thing running through my mind.

I grab them both by the arm and pull them to the mattress curling them into my chest as we lie down to hide them from watching the massacre taking place outside. Julie's gripping onto me as hard as she can.

"What are we gonna do?" The calmness in Tommy's voice is now gone.

"I dunno, sweetie."

"I'm scared." Julie's voice trembles with fear and exhaustion.

"I know. Me too."

My mind goes blank. I feel numb. I can't move.

All I can do is stare at the ceiling.

Then suddenly, a wasp crawls through a vent in the ceiling. Then another. And another. *Fuck!*

I'm not sure if it's motherly instincts or simply the will to survive, but a possible way out pops into my brain. It's not the safest route, but it will have to do. We're backed into a corner. Time is running out. I frantically jump out of bed and rummage through my purse looking for my keys.

"Mommy! What's wrong?!" Julie's voice is almost screeching.

"They're coming through the vents! We have to go. NOW!"

Tommy looks up. "Hoooollllyyy shit! How is that possible?!"

Julie screams. Not just a little bit. I mean ... she *screams* at the top of her lungs.

Tommy puts his hand over her mouth right as I yank the keys out of the bag.

"Let's go!" I put my hand on the doorknob. "Don't stop for anything. You get in the car no matter what. Even if there are some wasps in there, it's better than 10,000 of them coming at you at once. We have to make a run for it. We have to do this. You guys with me?!"

My directions cut right through to the kids, and they can't argue. All they can do is nod their heads in agreement.

I open the door trying to remain quiet and not disturb the wasps that are in the house. I inch my way to the garage door and open it with both kids trailing behind me and put my hand up like I'm in Black Ops telling them to hold their position. The garage door screeches as it opens to the hell waiting for us outside. Dozens of wasps scatter away from the noise, but some of them rush into the garage buzzing around frantically.

"This is it," I whisper to the kids and hit the key fob to make sure the doors are open.

We bolt for the car and don't stop. Tommy opens the back door behind the driver's side, and he pushes Julie into the car. The sound of the wasps intensifies as we get out into the open air. I shove Tommy into the car and slam the door shut.

Somehow, I'm able to get into the driver's seat and close my door without being stung. I rub my hands through my hair and neck making sure I don't have any clinging to me.

"Are you guys okay?"

"Yeah, I think so." Tommy's panting like he just ran a mile.

I take one last look at Ben lying in the grass on his back with wasps still crawling on most of his lifeless body. It feels so wrong leaving him here. He forgave me for what I did. He didn't leave me behind. I don't think I can do this to him even if he is dead. How can I leave him after everything we've been through?

"Mom!" Tommy's voice sounds muffled, and I can barely hear him as my grief overtakes me. "We have to go!"

I start to bawl and bang at the steering wheel.

"Ahhhhhh!"

Both kids put their hands on my shoulder trying to calm me down. With my head leaning on the wheel, I look over at the ground where the wasps are still coming in and out of their nest in the ground. Who would have thought a huge nest would be underneath the ground there? We never know what's lying right below us in the shadows ready to come out. I guess some things are meant to stay buried, and some things are meant to come to the surface.

I drive away as fast as I can and look in the rearview mirror one last time at the hell we're leaving behind. I make a right out of our driveway onto the main road and head back toward town to get help.

I want to ask the kids if they're okay again, but I know. They aren't okay. None of us will ever be okay again.

As we drive in silence, I hear it—the faint buzz of a wasp.

THE
CHAIR

The Chair

The electricity pierced through his body streaming from his nipples to every fiber of his being. He couldn't hear himself scream through the electric shock flowing through his body. Sweat and blood poured from his face, interlaced with tears and agony. He didn't know how much longer he could hold out. The last thing he wanted to do in this world was give up the big secret. It would put his best friend in jail and probably ruin his own life. The punches to the face. The kicks to the groin. His fingernails peeled off one by one with needle-nose pliers. Everything they'd done to him up until this point was somewhat manageable, but the electricity ... oh, the electricity. It was something he couldn't handle—his breaking point.

"All you have to do is give us a name. It's that simple." The man sat with his finger on the power button.

"Alright! Alright! Jesus! I'll give you the damn name. Just ... please. Stop." His voice became weak and defeated like so many others before him.

"Well ... let's hear it." The man got close to his face, egging him on to confess.

"Ed Leary! Ed *fucking* Leary! He runs the prostitution ring in Somerset. It was his idea. He's the boss."

They already knew the name they were looking for thanks to the researchers. They only needed to hear him say it.

"Are youuu sureee?" The man drew out his words for effect.

"Yes! It's fucking him. Please, don't kill me! I have a wife and three kids. *Please!*"

Suddenly, the walls started to transform into a honeycomb pattern. Then the ceiling and floors. Everything around the room vanished almost in an instant, including the interrogator. It was like he had never even been there.

"What's going on? What the hell is this?" The man's face turned from defeat and pain to confusion as he blinked his eyes, hoping they would put the room back together for him.

A door opened, revealing a bright white light glaring through, blinding the man. A shadow filled the doorway, and the host entered the room. The master of ceremonies. The creator and conductor of the greatest game show ever created—*The Chair*. Normal, everyday people are plucked from their lives to expose their biggest and darkest secrets. The audience at home sits on the edge of their seat wondering if the contestant will snitch on themselves or someone they know. If they snitch, they lose and go to jail. If they hold out, they win and get released scot-free— all they have to do is tough it out during their virtual torture session.

"Well, well, well, Mr. Jacobsen. I'm so disappointed in you." The melodic sound of the crowd humming "boo" echoed through the room. "I think *everyone* is disappointed in you."

"Who the hell are you? What's going on?!" The man tried to wriggle out of his restraints without any luck.

"You don't watch too much TV now do you, Mr. Jacobsen?"

He didn't respond and continued his efforts to escape from his restraints.

"You're on a game show called *The Chair*! Now, wave hello to our audience and everyone watching at home."

The man continued to try to squirm out of his predicament, but there wasn't anywhere for him to go even if he did get out.

"Oops. My apologies. It doesn't look like you can wave with your arms restrained to the chair there." The host giggled his signature, sinister chuckle, his whitened teeth beaming across his spray-tanned, orange face. This was one of his favorite parts of the show—toying with the guest, especially when they've snitched. "Let's take a moment to recap first. Shall we?"

The sound of the audience clapping echoed through the studio confusing Mr. Jacobsen even more.

"Your best friend ... what was his name? Ah, yes! Ed Leary! This gentleman has been running a prostitution ring out of his secret estate for the past year and a half. His wife and kids don't know about it. His coworkers and friends never picked up any of the clues or got pulled into his little secret. No! You were the *only* one he trusted. Some best friend you are. And now, you've spilled the beans. And with only forty-eight seconds remaining!" The audience filled the room with "hmms" and "ahhs" as they reacted to the host's recap. "That's one of the closest margins we've seen on this show! That's all you had left, and you'd be a free man."

The emcee of torture stood silent, letting the news sink in for a moment. The look of terror someone has on their face when they've realized they've made a huge mistake now sat on the face of Mr. Jacobsen. He sank his head in embarrassment, finally noticing the clamps from the battery were no longer pinching his nipples. His fingernails were intact. There weren't any open wounds on his face from the punches. The blood no longer mixed in with his sweat. It was all a rouse.

"I have to say," Clark continued, "kudos to our audience for voting to select such a great torture device to get us to the finish line!"

The audience cheered loudly, knowing they had a hand in helping the bad guy squeal.

The game show had access to one of the most advanced pieces of technology on the market. They bought it through a startup company that cashed out early, giving them sole rights to their setup. A true virtual reality experience makes the user feel like they're experiencing everything in front of them. Once a subject sits in the chair, they're injected with their patented nano-chip that taps into every major system in the body. From there, they can control every feeling and experience the person goes through while they're in the chair. They have complete control of everything they hear, feel, smell, taste, and see. The five senses are artificially manipulated to create the perfect nightmare. They're even able to tap into what the subject sees and display it for the audience at home and in the studio.

"It's safe to say you won't be going home anytime soon." His signature chuckle filled the room. "Do you have anything you'd like to tell the audience?"

"Fuck you." Mr. Jacobsen barely managed to get the words out of his mouth. Despite no physical harm coming to him, he was exhausted. Mentally drained and defeated.

"Well, that's certainly not a nice thing to say to our audience. What if your wife and kids are watching at home? Would you want them to hear that awful language? Do you have anything you'd like to say to *them*?"

Mr. Jacobsen sat in silence. His hanging head swayed to the side, and he passed out. The lights began to dim, and a spotlight focused on the host.

"Well, it looks like that does it for today's show, folks. Tune in next week to find out what happens with this Mr. Ed Leary. And always be ready for another contestant to show us if they've got the itch to snitch." A few big men entered the room and started unstrapping Mr. Jacobsen from his chair. They carried his limp body in the background of the shot as the host wrapped things up. "I'm Clark Richmond, and I thank you for tuning in to the greatest game show on Earth. Until next time …" He waved to the crowd and ended with his signature line, "Don't do anything I wouldn't do!"

The lights faded to black as the feed cut out.

Clark unbuttoned the top button of his dress shirt and loosened his tie as he walked backstage. "What in the actual fuck, Doug?!" he yelled through his mic still connected to the producer.

"What's wrong? That was great." Doug's voice streamed through Clark's earpiece.

"You made him pass out too early, you stupid son of a bitch! We should have asked him how much he participated in the ring. He may have known more than just the damned secret. He could have been involved more, or maybe even be a customer for Christ's sake!"

"Sorry, boss. I didn't see it in the notes."

"Well, you're fired! Same goes for the person who provided the show notes! You're all fucking fired!"

This wasn't the first time Clark had hit his staff with empty threats. Doug would still direct the next show like he always had, but rest assured, he'd remember to double-check the notes and double-check the right time to inject the subject with the tranquilizer.

Clark stormed out of the interrogation room and headed to his dressing room. He sat at the makeup chair and pulled out some pepsi from his pocket. And no, it wasn't the famous soft drink. Technical upgrades in virtual reality weren't the only human advancement in recent history. Porn and drugs were always at the forefront of human progression. Pepsi was basically a new cocaine. An advanced version that prevented overdoses. It was impossible to take too much, and with the threat of death no longer looming over the famous drug from the 1980s, it had been rebranded to Coke's adversary—Pepsi.

Almost everyone was on this stuff, especially celebrities and high-profile citizens like Clark. He took a device from his pocket that looked like a straw with a straightened edge on one side. It allowed him to use the straight edge to shuffle the pepsi around into nice, neat lines, and then, he turned it around to snort the powdered substance through the tube.

This stuff was so popular people even did it out in the open. The government tried to make it a controlled substance, but everyone protested. This led to the Great Riots, and ultimately the diminishment of law enforcement in America. It was still around but lacked the necessary funding to make an impact in communities. Outsourcing to private investigators skyrocketed. The creation of *The Chair* was a lifesaver for law enforcement. Not only because it helped catch bad guys, but it also deterred criminals from committing crimes.

Clark didn't even flinch when a showrunner lightly knocked on his door.

"Mr. Richmond?" A hesitation emanated from the young girl's voice.

"What?!" he yelled back without taking his eyes off his reflection in the mirror.

"You're wanted in the control room."

"Ha!" His signature chuckle shortened to one note. "Let me guess. They sent *you* down here because the rest of them were too scared to come straight to me."

The young girl stood silently, holding her clipboard, and stared down at her toes.

"They can wait. Come here for a moment."

A look of terror plastered the young girl's face.

"Jesus! I'm not going to hurt you. Just because I host the most vicious game show in history doesn't mean I torture everyone I meet."

She walked over to him with hesitation, and all the while, he kept his gaze on himself in the mirror.

"Pull out your phone."

She did.

"Read them to me."

"Sorry ... what do you want me to read?"

"The comments! The damned comments from the piss ants you call a society."

She fumbled to open one of her social apps, and her heart rate increased as she began to read the comments from both Clark's fans and his enemies.

"You piece of shit! How do u live with urself?!"

"Clark Richmond is a GOD among men!"

"I wish I could put you in that chair myself. How would you like it if someone ruined your life you son of a bitch?!"

"Thank u for keeping our streets clean Mr. Richmond! U R a hero!"

"Kill yourself!!! The devil has a special place in hell reserved for you!"

The young girl kept on for several minutes. There were thousands of comments to read, and Clark soaked up every one of them, especially the negative ones. Yeah, some people loved him, but the ones who hated him ... that's where the money flowed from. The weaving of sheer anger from his enemies with the acclimation from his followers made him feel fulfilled and continued to bring in higher and higher ratings. Discourse equaled ratings. He loved sowing seeds of friction for the plebeians of society to fuel those ratings.

As the nervous showrunner continued to read, the smile on Clark's face extended further and further as the bright bulbs from the mirror accentuated his masked face of spray-tan, makeup, teeth whitener, and plastic surgery.

01000100 01100001 01110010 01101011 00100000 01001101 01100001 01110100 01110100 01100101 01110010

Clark burst through the conference room door to a sea of producers, writers, and other members of the game show crew. Now that he had calmed himself from the huge mistake his producer Doug made by injecting Mr. Jacobsen with the tranquilizer before Clark could question him about his participation in the prostitution ring, he had already completely forgotten about firing Doug. He was always soon to forget his empty threats.

"Everyone keep your panties on. You all look like you're about to shit a brick." Clark sat at the head of the table, clicking his heels onto the edge of the conference room table.

"Sorry for jumping the gun on the transition, Boss." There was a shake in Doug's voice.

"Just don't let it happen again. What's next?"

"We're continuing to monitor this Ed Leary guy. Looks like he purchased a one-way ticket to Mexico right after the show ended. We've got eyes on him, and he's packing his bags as we speak."

"Good. Can we squeeze him in for tomorrow?"

"Yeah ... I think so. The I-Team is in position, waiting for him to head to his car."

The I-Team stood for "Intercept Team." A group of about four to five men who intercepted targets for the show. With the depletion of the police force in the city over several years, including a major lack of funding, the city was more than happy to grant permission to allow the studio to use its money and resources to help capture bad guys. Each case had to be approved by the city before any actions were taken. Luckily, this was a tactic they had used dozens of times in the past. Get the friend to snitch, then hit the target. It created a storyline. A flow and build-up to the big target.

"Let me know when he's secure. I want to get this recorded ASAP. I have big plans this weekend."

Those "big plans" included copious amounts of pepsi and prostitutes. Not the sleazy kind Ed Leary pushed out into the market. No, these were high-end prostitutes reserved for high rollers. In fact, Clark was getting some money on the side from this particular ring for helping them take out the competition in the show today.

"What's next?"

One of the newer, less experienced writers raised his hand to chime in with his pitch.

"Don't raise your fucking hand! Jesus. This isn't grade school." Clark snapped his fingers, trying to recall the new writer's name.

"Jimmy, sir. My name's Jimmy."

"Well, Jiminy fucking Cricket. What'dya got?"

"Ummm ... yeah, so ... there's a lady who works down at the city's Waste Management department. She ... uhh ... she's been embezzling money into a private account. She's using the money to go on cruises with her boyfriend, and I think ..."

"Stop!" Clark held up his hand. "Where's the violence?"

"Uhh ... yeah. No violence, sir."

"We need *blood*, people! You all know the ratings drop if we don't have a violent crime on our hands. Who the fuck cares about some lady stealing a few bucks from the city. Pass it off to the police and let them deal with that nonsense. If it doesn't involve blood or sex, the audience will lose interest. Fucking amateur hour!"

Jimmy sunk back into his seat, hoping he could turn invisible to hide from the embarrassment.

"Anyone else got any bright fucking ideas?"

The group was hesitant to bring anything else to the table and sat silent.

"For fuck's sake. Do I have to do everything around here? Find something quick. Once we get Leary in here, we only have two more contestants in the queue. The studio's already up my ass about our ratings slipping last quarter. If we drop one more fucking percent, you all will be out on the streets. We need something *big*. Got it?!"

He stormed out of the conference room leaving the group with a sigh of relief now that they could unclench their assholes. They quickly got to work on a potential project that could give their boss exactly what he was asking for.

Created with Sketch.

On his way out of the office, the brisk cold air of the city rushed in between buildings and smacked him in the face. Clark despised the city, especially everyone who inhabited it. He stepped past a homeless man lying against the side of the building using it to block the wind from hitting his body. It revolted Clark knowing the dirt and grime from unkempt humans like this littered the streets. He was sure the blocks of cement he stepped on were soaked with urine, tainting his Italian leather loafers as he walked to his car. He made a note to clean them when he arrived at his uptown condo overlooking the city he abhorred.

That hate helped fuel his passion for his game show. It made all the hard work worthwhile knowing he was cleaning these streets up one episode at a time. He also liked the idea of having a bodyguard to protect him and continue his quest to clean up this scummy city. After Clark snapped his fingers, the bodyguard quickly picked up the homeless man and carried him around the corner into the alley, gave him a few good whacks, and told him to stay away from the building. Clark watched gleefully from the car, thankful he didn't have to do the job himself and potentially get blood on his custom-fitted suit. He preferred to deal with the fake blood from The Chair.

It was a short drive to the condo. He could walk the few blocks to get to his building, but he wouldn't be caught dead walking the streets. There were too many people who wanted him dead, especially past contestants who wanted revenge. One guy who had recently been released from prison for sexually assaulting underage girls tried to stab him on his way out of the office only a few weeks ago. Thankfully, his bodyguard tackled the guy before he even got close. This was normal for Clark. It kept him on his toes and certainly kept his bodyguard busy.

He stepped into his condo, took off his shoes, and began to unbutton his dress shirt as he walked into the kitchen. The place was pristine with no trace of dirt, dust, or germs. Clark made sure the cleaning company kept his place as spotless as a kitchen in a Mr. Clean commercial. It didn't take long for him to end up on his couch with a glass of wine and his finger ready to dial his contact.

"Dimitri!" Clark didn't even give him a chance to say hello when he answered his call. "How'd you like the show?"

"You haven't reached the finish line yet, my friend." Dimitri's Russian accent sounded harsh through the phone almost more than it did in person.

"We got Leary in our sights. Should have him in custody tonight."

"Every day that fucker has girls on the streets, I'm losing money."

"I'm on it."

"You better be."

"Oh, and one more thing."

"Ugh. You Americans. Always greedy for more."

"I just want a girl." Clark couldn't wait until the weekend for pepsi and prostitutes.

"Fine. You want the usual?"

"No, no. Nadia's old news. Got any new girls for me?"

"Yeah, I have one that just came off the boat. Katia. Nice and fresh for you."

"Great. Have her bring some pepsi."

Clark hung up the phone quickly and grabbed his tablet. He used it to lower the lighting to a dim ambiance and selected "Hungry Like a Wolf" by *Duran Duran* to blast through his speakers. With another snort of pepsi, Clark was well on his way to having a great night.

He was anxious to get started with this new girl, Katia. After only twenty minutes, restless energy overtook his body as he grew more impatient with every second ticking away. Despite his impatience, he was still on cloud nine. Another successful show in the books (even though he felt it could have been better), and Ed Leary was in his sights. One more torturous interrogation and he'd get paid almost an entire year's salary. Talk about killing two birds with one stone. His plans were finally coming to fruition.

Usually, the wait for one of Dimitri's girls only took about fifteen minutes. It was now up to almost forty-five since he made his request. Clark grabbed his phone and started to type furiously.

"Where's my fucking girl?!"

A knock at the door was muffled by the loud 80s pop music screeching through the speakers. He casually walked to the door and opened it without looking through the peephole. For Clark, everything went dark in an instant as he was injected with a tranquilizer shot.

01000100 01100001 01110010 01101011 00100000 01001101 01100001 01110100 01110100 01100101 01110010

He woke up restrained to a chair. *How fucking ironic?* he thought. But then, the reality of the situation kicked in. He didn't know what the hell was going on, and his date with Katia was most likely not going to happen at this point. *Where the hell am I? Who the hell kidnapped me?*

Then it clicked. Dimitri was cold on the phone. Much colder than he normally is. Something must have gone wrong with the deal. No way this was the cops. They don't use these tactics—that's what they pay Clark for.

Am I in ... The Chair? he thought. *There's no way. That's* my *chair.*

A bald, burly man walked through the door and laid out a leather case of knives, clamps, and other torture devices. Clark knew this strategy all too well from his show. It's the build-up. The anticipation of the pain makes it all that much more excruciating. The man pulled out one of the knives and started sharpening it. The *cling* sound with every sharpening stroke pierced Clark's ears and made him wince.

"You don't think I know my own fucking show? What the fuck is going on, Doug?!" Clark called out to his producer, hoping to strike one last ounce of fear into him. He knew it was The Chair ... *his* Chair.

"Mr. Richmond," the bald man spoke in a Russian accent, "I would say this won't take long, but then I'd be lying."

"Okay, I'll play along, jerk off. Where's Dimitri? I want to talk to Dimitri."

"He's not available right now. Please leave a message. Beep!" Baldy slapped Clark across the face, and you could see the lights go out in his eyes for a moment. It almost knocked him into another dimension. But really, it gave him a hint of a doubt this could actually be real. It felt *so* real.

"Fuck!" Clark yelled out in pain. "I want to see Dimitri. He wouldn't be programmed into the system. Prove to me this is real. I want to see Dimitri. Now!" Clark tried to wriggle out of the restraints.

Baldy slapped Clark again, causing his lip to bleed and drip down onto his white dress shirt. "Tsk tsk tsk. I wouldn't be making threats in your position, Mr. Richmond."

The pain from the slap caused the entire left side of his face to tingle like he got pegged in the face with a dodgeball. Then, Baldy stomped on his ankle breaking several bones.

"Ahhh!!!" Clark screamed out in agony. He dropped his head, causing more blood to spill from his lip as he continued to scream out in pain. A part of him was completely sure he was in The Chair until that moment. A shred of doubt still lingered in his brain, but if anyone could tell, it would be him. He finally gained his composure after a few deep breaths. "If this is in fact real, the deal is over if you don't let me fucking go. Leary will continue his operation, and I'll come after you and that fucking snake Dim—"

"We're just getting started. Maybe you can stop making threats and tell me how you're fucking us."

"What are you talking about?" Clark licked at the blood dripping from the side of his mouth. "Doug! What the fuck are you doing?! Get me out of this thing!"

Baldy winced in confusion. "There's no Doug here, Mr. Richmond. Only you, me, and my tools. I've seen your show several times, which is going to make this all the more fun for me. Now, let's walk through it from the beginning. Tell me how your deal with Dimitri started."

"Fuck you. I'm not saying shit. I know you can hear me, Doug!"

"Let me make this real clear to you, *Clark*." Baldy held back his Russian accent when saying his name to make it sound as American as he could. "He knows you're fucking him on this deal. We know you're talking to the cops. Now," he started sharpening his knife again, "tell me about your deal with Dimitri. Start from the beginning and don't ask me another question." He gently dug the tip of his knife into Clark's neck to let him feel the sharpness. To feel the *realness* of its steel. And that's exactly how it felt to Clark. *Real.*

"Okay, okay. Fine."

Baldy returned to his tools and began sharpening the knife as a small stream of blood trickled down Clark's neck. The high-pitched screech from the sharpening blade rolled up Clark's spine with each stroke. "Dimitri called me out of the blue one day. He told me he had a tip for the show. Offered up his competition. This Ed Leary guy was running a prostitution ring on the lower-east side of the city. Everyone knows the Russians run the east side, and he wanted them out."

"Good. Keep going." Baldy ran the sharpened blade up Clark's forearm only grazing the skin.

"I asked him why he didn't do it himself. He told me he had other matters to attend to. You know?"

"You're not following the rules, Mr. Richmond." The bald man grabbed his pinky finger, pulled it to the side, and cut it off with one swipe.

Again, Clark screamed out.

"Stop asking questions! Pinky promise me you'll tell me *everything*." The bald man chuckled as he held the dismembered appendage in front of Clark's face. "Pretend I don't know anything and stop asking questions."

"Jesus Christ! You fucking bastard! What did I say?"

Another question.

This time the other pinky finger came off.

The screaming continued for a moment until Baldy punched Clark across the face with full force. The screaming stopped, and his head hung low as more blood spilled onto his shirt, and streams of blood dripped down the arms of the chair from his fingers. Clark almost called the bald man another name but decided against it and continued to hang his head.

Baldy grabbed Clark's hair and pulled his head back, but Clark's hair wasn't actually hair. His toupee ripped off his scalp, showing the typical male-pattern baldness you'd see in a middle-aged man.

The Russian laughed deep from within his belly. "Now we are both alike. See?" Baldy lifted Clark's head and squeezed his cheeks. "You Americans are so self-absorbed. Always worried about what others think of you." He walked away from his subject back to his tools, giving Clark a moment to regain his composure so he could continue to spill his beans.

After a few moments, Baldy asked, "Are you ready to continue?"

"I'll tell you everything. Please ... don't hurt me."

Baldy didn't say another word and grabbed a

scalpel, waving it at Clark in a playful way.

"Okay. Okay." Clark swallowed and took a deep breath before continuing. "So, the Russians are at war with the Choi Family who run the west side of the city." *Two fucking communists using this dirty American city as a war ground*, Clark thought to himself. "Dimitri had his men focused on taking out Choi and wanted me to step in to take care of Leary. His prostitution ring funded his war against Choi, and he was losing market share with Leary going in with a lower cost."

"So how are you fucking, Dimitri? I know you have a plan to take him out, too. *The Chair* always finds a way to go up the ladder, no?" He placed the scalpel on Clark's forearm and applied enough pressure to draw blood.

"Yes! Yes! We always go up the ladder. But we made a deal. We made a *fucking* deal, and it was going to stop at Leary!'

"I don't believe you."

The man swiped across Clark's forearm creating a small slit.

"Ahhhh!" Clark screamed out.

"Are you sure?"

"Yes! I swear to fucking God!"

Another slit.

"Stop! Stop!"

Another slit.

This went back and forth for a few minutes until Clark had micro-slits up and down both forearms, creating red lines across his skin. His arms looked like potatoes au gratin sliced every quarter inch, but instead of a cheese topping, it was a creamy marina sauce of blood. Tears streamed down his face, and he was losing the will to even scream at this point. He was close. Almost ready to reach the breaking point.

"You're not telling me everything here, Mr. Richmond." Baldy wiped the dripping blood from the scalpel with a towel. "Like I said, I've seen your show many times. You always play games. It's what you do."

"I'm not ..."

"You Americans think you're so smart. You think you're above everyone else." Baldy closed in on Clark and was only inches from his face. "You're nothing but a *suka*. A *bitch*."

Clark spat in his face. A mixture of blood, sweat, and tears streamed down the man's face. He slowly started to undo the restraints holding Clark to the chair with a menacing grin.

"What are you doing?" Clark's voice turned to a whimper. "Stop. Please!"

Baldy dragged Clark out of the chair toward the corner of the room where there was a long trough filled with water. He threw Clark's face into the water and held him under while screams softly echoed from underneath the surface.

He pulled him up from the water.

"This isn't a game, Clark!"

Put him back under.

Pull him out.

"This is real life, Clark!"

Put him back under.

Pull him out.

"Dimitri knows you're fucking him!"

Put him back under.

Clark's bloody arms flailed in the air, trying to grab at the hand on the back of his head forcing him down. His legs kicked back and forth, scuffing the floor with his Italian leather shoes. Then, he stopped all at once.

Baldy threw Clark onto his back, and his bald head hit the concrete floor. His unconscious body lay wet, bloody, and limp without any breath escaping his mouth. He quickly slammed his fist down on Clark's chest, and a fountain of water came spraying out of Clark's mouth as he searched for his next breath while thinking it could be his last.

The Russian grabbed a cinder block leaning against the wall and walked over to Clark lying on the floor. "This is last chance for you, my friend." He held the cinder block high over his head ready to drop it on Clark's face to end his life. The light from above reflected off Clark's forehead. The orange from the spray tan ran down his face, now interlaced with blood and the water from the trough. All the plastic surgery, teeth whitening, and other expensive masks Clark used to cover up who he really was were about to be destroyed by forty pounds of compacted cement and ash.

"Alright. I'll tell you everything." Clark's voice

now lowered to a defeated tone. "*Please.* Put the block down, and I'll tell you everything."

Baldy dropped the block next to Clark's head and dragged him up into the chair. He didn't say a word. Only stared into his eyes in anticipation, waiting for him to either snitch or mess up again.

"I've been playing both sides this whole time. I knew Dimitri would ask me to take care of Leary. He's always asking me to clear out his garbage. But I've also been working with Choi to take out Dimitri. Once we took out Leary, we were going to turn our focus to Dimitri and the Russians. We have everything laid out for the cops to take over and put him out of business. Choi was going to pay me double what Dimitri was offering, plus I'd get the payout from Dimitri for taking care of Leary."

"Wow. Sounds like a big payday for you." Baldy laughed sarcastically.

"I won't take any of the money. I can help you take out the Choi Family. I can be a double agent for you guys. I'll do it for free. Just please don't kill me!"

"Unfortunately, we already have everything we need on Choi, Mr. Richmond."

"I can get you more. I know people. Please!"

"Leary is already in custody. Now you've implicated both Dimitri and Choi. Our forces are working with your I-Team to intercept all parties as we speak."

"Wait. What are you saying?"

The room gradually turned into the blank

honeycomb backdrop from the game show, and the Russian interrogator disappeared. Clark's eyes refocused, and he noticed the marks on his arm and all the pain was now gone. He wiggled his pinky fingers still attached to his hand. A younger man in a sharp suit and an even whiter smile than Clark walked into the room.

How could it be, Clark thought. *It's not possible!*

"What a roller coaster of a ride that was. Eh, Mr. Richmond?" The young man chuckled a deep laugh from his chest.

"What is this?!"

"What? You don't recognize your own set, Mr. Richmond?"

A mocking laugh from the audience filled the room along with claps and cheers.

"There's no way. I don't ... there's just no way." Clark placed his head into his hands and began rubbing his bald head back and forth trying to make sense of it all. "Doug! Doug!? Where the hell are you?! You're fucking fired! You'll never work another day in this town!"

"Haha! I'm sorry Mr. Richmond, but you're mistaken. I believe it is *you* who will never work another day in this town. Well, at least not on this show. Haha!" That deep chuckle almost mocked Clark's menacing laugh. "If you haven't figured it out already, I'm your replacement." Then turning to the camera, "My name's Hal Carson, and I'll be your new host of the most exciting game show in television history—*The Chair*!"

The audience clapped and cheered furiously. Clark sat in the chair with a dumbfounded look on his face, still trying to piece together how this could have happened to him.

"What's the line you always ended your shows with, Mr. Richmond?"

Clark continued his blank stare.

"'Don't do anything I wouldn't do!' Yes, that's it! Haha!" Hal's chuckle lined up with the laughing from the audience. "I'm not so sure that was great advice considering everything we've learned today. Guess I'll need to come up with something new. Hmmm ..." Hal placed his index finger on his chin in deep thought. "I got it! How about—'Don't do anything *Clark* wouldn't do?' Yes! That sounds catchy enough."

Two large men walked through the door just as Clark tried to lunge at Hal. They carried him out of the room as he kicked and screamed in anger and frustration. His life wasn't over, but it certainly wouldn't be the same again.

"Well, that does it for tonight's historic evening here on The Chair," Hal continued. "Until next time, don't do anything *Clark* wouldn't do!"

01000100 01100001 01110010 01101011 00100000 01001101 01100001 01110100 01110100 01100101 01110010

Clark sat in a white room with a gray metal table and a wide mirror where he knew people were sitting behind it watching him, but he could only see his reflection. He looked like a new man, but not in a good way. The absence of his toupee showcased the top of his bald head. The spray tan was no longer an orange layer on his face. The white in his teeth faded darker and darker with each day he was held in his cell. He twitched, cocking his head to the side every ten seconds or so, and huge bags had formed under his eyes, both caused by withdrawal from the pepsi. It turned out to be the only thing he wished for besides getting out of this hell hole. Not even the prostitutes were worth more to him at this point.

The interrogations didn't stop after he left The Chair. The police bombarded him with questions about Leary, Dimitri, and the Choi Family. He didn't lie once. With nothing to lose, he figured, why not? Dimitri or Choi would get to him whether he landed in jail or out on the streets. He was a dead man either way. The host of a game show about snitches and secrets was now the victim of his own setup.

A young woman with a gold police badge dangling from her neck walked into the room and slammed down a large file of papers onto the metal table, snapping Clark from his daze at his reflection.

"Well, you did it, Mr. Richmond. We had the basics nailed down, but you gave us the details to put these guys away."

"Who?" He responded without a dose of animation in his voice. The sound of a man who had been defeated.

"All of them. Each and every one of them is either behind bars or on their way there. Leary. Dimitri and his crew. The Choi Family. All of 'em. Thanks to you."

Clark sat motionless and without expression.

Detective Ortiz slid a piece of paper across the table and placed a pen next to it.

Clark removed his gaze from the mirror finally and looked down at the paper. "What's this?"

"The terms of your release."

"My release?" Clark sat up and scanned the paper. "Seriously?"

"Yes, sir. Due to your cooperation and support that led to the arrest of dozens of men who will no longer abuse and subjugate women, we're issuing your release effective immediately. Including your many years of service to help clean up our community, consider this a thank you. If you wish to speak with your lawyer to go over the terms, we can arrange for—"

"No, no," Clark interrupted and signed the paper. "I'll take it."

"We'll be keeping an eye on you, Mr. Richmond. Follow me."

Detective Ortiz walked Clark to the front desk, and a man with the same male-patterned baldness gave him his belongings—his wallet, belt, pepsi straw, keys, and cell phone. Clark signed for the items, nodded to Detective Ortiz, and walked out of the building a free man.

With all of Dimitri's crew and the Choi Family locked up, he was truly a free man. He wouldn't have to worry about any retaliation, at least for the next three to five years. People on the street walked around him without a second glance. He realized no one recognized him anymore without his mask. The people of the city either hated or loved the bright-smiled host of The Chair, but the *real* Clark Richmond was unsuspecting and fit into the background of the city.

After a few months without being able to land another job, Clark was thrown out onto the streets he despised. Unable to pay his rent and basic living needs, he became a man of those streets. He fell from the top all the way to the very bottom. But he still had his life. His existence in this world was all that mattered. To a self-centered sociopath, that's all he wanted. An existence. It didn't matter that he became the type of person he used to despise and even had his bodyguard rough up from time to time. He was now that person, and he loved himself regardless.

He sat at the entrance of the studio he used to work at, watching the suited representatives of the community walk in and out of the revolving door. His beard now fully concealed his face from any recognition of the man who warned the country not to do anything he wouldn't do.

Coins clinked in his plastic cup by his feet as a young girl placed some change in there for him. He only needed a few more bucks, and he would be able to score some more pepsi. He twitched from the withdrawal of not having the drug for almost a week now and shut his eyes for a moment.

When he opened them, Hal Carson stood in front of him with his bulging bodyguard standing behind his right shoulder. Hal thumbed through a wad of cash in his hand, looking for the correct bill. He plucked a twenty out of the thick roll and placed it in Clark's cup.

"Here you go, sir," Hal spoke with empathy and leaned down to eye level with Clark. "There's a homeless shelter a few blocks south of here. Tell them I sent you, and you should get a warm meal and bed for the night."

Clark looked up in astonishment. It was obvious Hal didn't even recognize him. He sat with his mouth agape.

As Hal stood and began to walk away, he looked down at him and said, "Don't do anything Clark wouldn't do!"

DEMI

Demi

Demi lived on her computer. She had an obsession—like most people—with a game she created called Worlds where a player could create any world they desired. It was something precious to her, and she wasn't sure anyone would like it. Still, she ended up releasing it to the masses without any help from a big company. One young girl created and distributed a video game all on her own. Her popularity rose along with the game as the mysterious creator. Regardless, she stayed in her little hideaway, a.k.a. her apartment, where she didn't have to interact with anyone she didn't want to. Plus, everything was so bland and boring in her actual world. Why would she even want to live outside of Worlds?

The boredom of her reality made it easy for her to escape to her own little sanctuary. A place she could call home with characters who adored her—

well, most of them. She could use her imagination to create and manage countries or dive deep into the life of a single character. Artificial intelligence helped her manage her society by creating learned behaviors and giving her characters free will to make their own decisions. Even though these characters could make their own choices, she still knew what they would do because it was her program, and she ultimately had full control.

Thanks to her short, yet prestigious, career as a coder, it was easy for Demi to create Worlds. Of course, she was the top player in the game and well-known in the online community for having created her world within Worlds in only one week. No other programmer had ever been able to set up an entire world in that short amount of time. With little to no sleep during that week, she became a legend in Worlds. To put it in perspective, there was only one other gamer who came close to her one-week record, and he was just shy of a month. It just so happens he was also Demi's best friend, Adam.

Despite all the followers she had, Adam was the only person Demi had any kind of relationship with in the real world. And they had never even met in real life. There was no point. The real world was filled with uncomplicated and predictable people who bored Demi, so she shut herself away. She didn't even have windows in her apartment. Micro-meals were delivered to her so she didn't have to go to the market. All she had to do was pop them in the microwave for a few minutes and she had the nourishment she needed to manage her online world for the day. All her essentials and necessities for life were delivered to her door. The last time she stepped foot outside of her apartment was on her twentieth birthday two years ago.

A convo request from Adam popped up on Demi's screen while she was creating a new amusement park for her world. She switched on her headset to connect with him.

"Hey, Adam."

"Happy birthday!!"

"Thanks."

"Let me guess ... you're playing Worlds?"

"Of course."

"What are you working on today?"

"A new amusement park. Thought it would be nice to celebrate my birthday with some new rides. This new coaster I built has a drop where the riders are upside down during the free fall! I wish we had something like that in real life."

"Where do you come up with this shit?"

"I dunno. It just comes to me, I guess. You're pretty creative yourself."

"Not enough to build an entire world in a week like some people I know."

"Yeah. Yeah. I bet you could do it if you really wanted to."

"Staying up for pretty much an entire week straight? No, thank you."

A thick layer of silence hung over the line for a

minute as Demi continued to build her coaster. Adam was used to these trail-offs where Demi got so focused on her game that she barely knew what was happening around her.

"You really need to get out more. There's a new restaurant that opened up down the street from me. Wanna try it out?"

It had been two years since Demi had left her apartment. Two years she had known Adam and had never met him in person. Two years since she had seen another face in person. Even the people delivering her essentials never saw her—they left packages at the door, and she waited until they walked away before opening her door. In those two years, her world had existed for millions of years. A key feature of the game was being able to slow down or speed up time in the world you were building.

"No thanks. I was about to pop in a micro-meal. Besides, you live like an hour away."

"Take the train. You can bring your laptop and work on your world while you're on your way. C'mon! It's your birthday!"

"It's just another day to me, Adam. Plus, I have work to do tonight."

"Fine." Adam's voice sounded defeated and annoyed all at the same time. "Have a *great* birthday."

A sound in her headset signaled he had cut the convo.

Demi felt bad and sent him a message, "Sorry!

Call you later." Then she put the finishing touches on her new coaster. She could finally open her new amusement park, and it was the best present she could have given herself. Seeing the laughing faces of children running through the playground she built a few weeks ago, as well as the screaming faces on her new coaster, put a huge smile on her face.

She pushed her chair back and headed to the kitchen only a few feet away in her tiny apartment. Her bed sat on a loft above the kitchen, creating a two-level space. Earlier that morning when Demi had woken up, her bed automatically flipped up into the wall as soon as she got out of bed. Almost everything in her apartment had space-saving features and automatic settings based on her preferences and habits.

After placing her cup on the designated circle on her kitchen counter, water flowed from below and filled her cup while she put her last micro-meal in the microwave. Lasagna ready to eat in only one minute. The bottle of her gen-vitamins rattled as she picked it up to take her daily dose. The tiny pill gave her all the vitamins and minerals a person would need in a day.

Demi swiped the side of her counter and a holographic screen appeared above the counter displaying her most-used apps. After checking on her upcoming micro-meal delivery, she swiped to her bank account to check her funds. The holographic screen showed a small sum of money in bold at the top of the screen. She had used up almost all her funds keeping Worlds running. With all the popularity surrounding the game, it was booming with new creators every second. That meant more servers. More backup. More money. And the money flowing in was not keeping up with what was needed to keep the game running.

Her low bank account and depleting resources meant only one thing. She needed to do something if she wanted to save Worlds.

01000100 01100001 01110010 01101011 00100000 01001101 01100001 01110100 01110100 01100101 01110010

Demi despised the thought of money almost as much as the people who pined for it daily. They were always scratching and clawing for every morsel they could get their hands on, and it made her sick to her stomach. The free market seemed to be anything but free. It was a money grab for status, hierarchy, and power. Some at the top claimed they were doing it for the good of society. They wanted to claim their wealth so they could help give it back. Others went Robin Hood-style by taking from the rich to give to the poor.

However, creating a world without money seemed strange to Demi. She planned to have it be a main part of her society like her own world, but eventually, she wanted to figure out how to lead that society to be free of money. She may not even need to figure out a way. Despite her creativity, it was the one problem she couldn't solve in her game and in real life. But if she could get her AI algorithm right, there might be a way for it to create a path toward a society free of currency. In the early days of her world, there wasn't any money, so she knew it was possible.

Not only was her low bank account nipping at the front of her brain, but her low friend count was bothering her as well. It's usually in our time of need, we rely on friends and family the most. And Demi had no family. At least, not anymore. She hoped one day she might be able to build a family and create a life for a daughter or son that was better than the world she lived in. Her only friend was Adam, and he was probably still mad at her for blowing him off last night. It was her birthday after all. Shouldn't she be free to do whatever she wanted?

Regardless, a pain in her gut told her she should reach out to Adam and try to set things right. All these thoughts about family made her realize he was the closest thing she had to a family. She dumped the rest of her now cold tea in the sink and sat down at her computer. "Call Adam," she commanded, and the call started to ring through her speakers.

Nothing. No answer.

The final ring faded, and a female, computer-generated voice stated Adam was unavailable. She began typing a note to him. Leaving voicemails made her cringe.

Adam. I'm really sorry about last night. I get in a mood on my birthday because I hate it so much. I don't want to grow old and wish I could be frozen in time. I woke up this morning and realized I wanted to be with you last night. I actually wish I had left my apartment and met you at the restaurant ... if you can believe that. I get caught up in my own little world. It's the most important thing to me. I know that's not a surprise to you, but maybe this will be. You're the most important person in the world to me. I love our friendship and honestly don't know what I'd do without you. Can I make it up to you? Please?!?!

She hit send on the message after re-reading it and fixing a few minor mistakes. Demi usually didn't correct her spelling mistakes on a simple text message, but this was an important one. Her ruffled rag of hair dangled in front of her face as she lowered her head into her hands, hoping Adam would respond soon.

A few minutes passed as she sat waiting in anticipation for him to respond. Her mouse hovered over the Worlds app for a minute until she clicked on it. She checked her friends list and saw Adam was offline. He was the only person she followed in the game even though she had millions following her. Everyone wanted to see what the creator of the game would create. Viewers could log in to view that person's world, and with the right permissions, they could even participate in someone else's world. Demi had that feature turned off for her world, though. No way she would let an outsider jump into her safe space. That was a feature she created specifically for Adam to join her world—and he was the only one.

As soon as that thought crossed her mind, Adam called her. She picked up before the first ring even finished.

"Adam. I am *sooo* sorry. I was such a jerk last night. I can't believe you put up with me and I ..."

"Woah. Demi, chill." His voice sounded strained and lethargic. "It's not even six in the morning. What are you doing up so early?"

"I couldn't sleep. Plus, I couldn't stop thinking about how much of a moron I was to you yesterday. You try to do this nice thing for me, and I blow you off. Then, shit hits the fan, and I just don't know what to do. I tried ..."

"Wait. Wait. What do you mean 'shit hit the fan'?"

"I'm broke, Adam. I went to refill my micro-meals, and my account was so low I almost couldn't place my order."

"I can spot you for some food."

"Thanks, but that's not the real problem."

"What could be worse than not having food to

eat? That seems pretty up there on the list of priorities to survive."

"I have a payment coming up for Worlds."

"Oh ..."

"Yeah ... I don't know what to do. If I can't make this payment, the storage, backup, security ... everything. It'll all be gone."

"What about all the money you're getting from users?"

"I'm basically giving it away for free. The one-time upfront fee is not keeping up with the amount of money needed to fund the game."

"Why don't you start charging a subscription? Or you could charge people for some of the add-ons?"

"No way!" Demi's voice boomed through Adam's headphones. If he wasn't fully awake before, he was now. "And be like one of those cheap money-grab games? Not a chance, Adam."

"Well then, what are you going to do?"

"I dunno. Is the birthday dinner offer still on the table? Maybe we could talk about it in person."

"Really?"

"Yeah."

"Okay, but I'm buying."

Demi laughed but also knew the seriousness behind the statement. Even though it was her idea for the make-up birthday dinner, she would be dead broke if she had to pay for the meal.

01000100 01100001 01110010 01101011 00100000 01001101 01100001 01110100 01110100 01100101 01110010

After spending over an hour in the bathroom trying to make herself look like she hadn't locked herself in her apartment for the last two years, Demi stood at her front door with her hand on the knob for another hour. Her head banged against the door as she tried to work up the courage to leave her apartment. She glanced back at the pile of micro-meal boxes in the corner of her kitchen, and the even bigger pile of laundry next to the washing machine. The messiness of her apartment never bothered her before, but at that moment, she realized it was time to grow up. She needed to save her game. She needed to get her life back together. And she needed Adam.

She took one deep breath and finally turned the knob to the door and took her first step outside her apartment in two years. Each step down the long narrow hallway became easier and easier. She pressed the button for the elevator and started to pull at the hairs at the corner of her right eyebrow —a nervous tic she had developed when stressed. When the doors opened, a young woman was standing inside. Demi hesitated.

"Going down?" the bright-eyed blonde asked.

Again, Demi hesitated.

The woman squinted her eyes, waiting for a response.

"Yeah. Sorry." Demi quickly stepped in before

the doors shut, secluded herself in the corner of the elevator, and crossed her arms to give herself a comforting hug. They sat in silence the entire way down, and the woman quickly left the elevator when the doors opened as she gave Demi a snarky glance.

Demi's anxiety continued to ramp up as she took her first step outside the apartment building into the bustling streets. The light from the sun blinded her. The noise from the cars and people passing by on their phones created a ringing in her ears. Her chest started to heave in and out. A man in a gray suit, yelling into his phone, bumped into her and shouted, "Watch it!"

The doorman to the building approached Demi and his mustache danced on his lip as he spoke. "Are you alright, young lady?"

Her breathing continued to sharpen into quick, splitting bursts. The veins by her temples began to pulsate making it feel like her head had its own heartbeat. Her palms began to sweat as her hands shook. She was having a panic attack and started to frantically pull on her eyebrow hairs.

"Can I help you with something?" He put his hand on her shoulder. It was the first time another human had touched her in two years. He helped her by taking deep breaths and encouraging her to do the same. Her breathing started to lengthen. In the middle of the busy sidewalk, these two strangers conducted a breathing exercise together. They began to breathe in harmony. The doorman gently rubbed her back with resounding comfort until a few minutes passed and she finally felt somewhat normal.

"Wow. Thank you." Demi put her hands on her knees, thankful the sudden panic attack had subsided.

"Is everything alright?"

"Yeah. Think I'm okay."

"Alright, well, where ya heading today? Do you want to come inside the lobby? I can grab you a water and a seat until you're feeling better."

"No, that's alright. I need to get to the train station."

"Well, that's simple enough. The stairs down to the train are right over there." The doorman pointed at the sign for the train only a half block from where they were standing. "You sure you're okay?"

"Yeah. Thanks to you." Demi smiled, wiping a few tears from her eyes and continued on her way, focusing on putting one foot in front of the other. Her eyebrow now had a noticeable gap from picking at it. She even counted her steps to keep her focus on something other than her anxiety scratching and clawing at her brain.

Once she got to her seat on the train and pulled out her laptop, she was back in her own little world and became more and more comfortable as the ride went on.

01000100 01100001 01110010 01101011 00100000 01001101 01100001 01110100 01110100 01100101 01110010

While the train ride to meet Adam was productive, she couldn't shake the feeling she was close to losing her world. For every tree she planted, the thought of waking up and not having her world to mold and observe would leave her empty. She could always start over. Maybe create a new game. But that didn't seem like it would be in the cards for her. She had put too much time and effort into this world. It wasn't perfect by any means. There was as much death, destruction, and mayhem as there was love, kindness, and structure. She needed the good and the bad to create some balance. That was alright to Demi. She didn't want a perfect world. It was hers, and she loved the drama as much as she loved the order and organization.

The train came to a stop, causing Demi to glance up from her computer sitting on her lap. This was the first time she had been out in the real world in two years. It was all the same. While busy and loud, it was so bland and boring compared to the world she had built. As she glanced out the window at the stale architecture, she wished she lived in her world. She tried that once though, and it didn't really work out. She never really felt a part of the world she created when she was in it—almost as much as she didn't feel a part of her real world. She knew she would always be their creator and could never be one of them. The same thought crossed her mind as a young businesswoman carrying a briefcase entered the train—*I could never be one of them.*

This woman was the antithesis of Demi's created world and the typical cardboard cutout of the world Demi inhabited. She had no distinguishing features and wore a dark business suit with her hair pulled back into a low ponytail. There was nothing exciting about her. No creativity. No spunk. Demi could tell just by looking at her that her personality was as boring as her appearance.

The train pulled away from the station and entered a tunnel. Demi saw herself in the glass window of the train and realized she had become a similar person. Her once short, blue hair was now grown out to a boring brown. Her skin was now a pale shade of nothing. Her clothes were dark and lacked any sense of fashion, especially compared to the people in her world she cherished so dearly. Even after spending over an hour getting ready, she was already starting to blend into her bland world.

She wondered what Adam might think of her. They had seen each other plenty on video chats, but seeing someone in person was different. Mainly, there weren't any filters she could use to hide her pale skin or enhance the features on her face.

The train stopped at the next station, and Demi

gathered her things, barely squeezing through the door as it was shutting. She wasn't used to traveling and almost missed her stop. Of course, right there waiting for her was Adam. He was much taller than she expected, having only seen him online. His bright blue eyes and blonde hair made him stand out from his surroundings. While the station was metallic and cold, he was bright and exuberant. Demi knew she had feelings for him solely based on him being the only person in the world she had any kind of relationship with, but seeing him in person changed her. Her world wasn't the only thing she cared about. After he gave her the biggest smile imaginable, she realized how much she loved him. It was truly love at first sight.

After walking toward each other, they both stopped before embracing. But then they hugged deeply for what felt like an hour to her, but it was more like a minute. All the anxiety and stress from that morning melted away. She thought she'd be nervous to meet him, but her palms were dry and her breathing was normal. Although her heart still seemed to be bumping in her chest, it was completely different than how it felt from the panic attack. All the pent-up feelings from the past two years of isolation were shredded in an instant.

"It's nice to see you in person ... finally." That big smile of his lit up the station.

"I didn't realize how tall you are."

"I didn't realize how short *you* are."

They both laughed and hugged again as Demi squeezed Adam's midsection as tight as she could, not wanting to let him go.

"Happy belated birthday!"

"Thanks." She looked down at her toes, still adapting to communicating in person.

Adam picked up her suitcase and grabbed her hand as they started walking. "I have a surprise to show you before we head to dinner."

"Really? I hate surprises."

"This is a good one. Trust me."

Adam grabbed onto Demi's hand, and they intertwined their fingers together. She was worried meeting in person would be more awkward, but he had a way of making her feel comfortable immediately. It was obvious to Demi this was more than a friendship, or at least that it could be, and she hoped Adam felt the same way.

They walked around a small pond and stopped at a bridge overlooking the murky water. Demi looked up at Adam and couldn't find a way to remove the smile from her face. Looking at him made her body feel infectious with lust—something she hadn't felt in a long time, or maybe ever.

"What's the surprise?

"Nope."

"C'mon! Please tell me!"

"I'd rather not."

"I need some good news, Adam. My game is falling apart. My *world* is falling apart. I'm like that duck over there." She pointed at a duck sitting in the pond staring off into space. "I may look all calm on the outside, but underneath the surface, my little duck feet are going a mile a minute."

"You look calm on the outside?" Adam chuckled and covered his mouth with his hand while he looked over at the duck.

Demi playfully punched him in the arm and gave him a serious stare that said, *this is my life, not some joke.*

"Alright, alright." He grabbed her by the hand. "Come with me."

They ditched the pond and started walking down a busy street with cars zooming by. People jogged past them in their tracksuits that all looked the same, and cyclists almost crashed into them as they walked. This was more stimulation than Demi had experienced outside of her apartment in more than two years. Her anxiety crept in, and she latched onto Adam, knowing he would protect her.

"Where are we going? I don't like surprises."

"It'll be fine. Look." He pointed to a coffee shop across the street. "There it is. Let's go."

Adam seemed to glide across the pavement as they crossed the street. They walked into the shop and sat at one of the stations. These CPU stations allowed the customer to order drinks directly from their screen. Adam put in an order for a black coffee, and Demi ordered a mint tea. A portion of the table slid open, and their drinks magically appeared within seconds of their order. A quick swipe across the screen brought up a search engine, and Adam typed "Evelyn Waters" into the search bar.

A picture of a dark-haired, blue-eyed woman appeared on the screen. She looked older than Demi and Adam, and according to her bio that popped up on the screen, she was 42 years old with no family and the CEO of a company called Interravision.

"Who's this?" Demi asked as she pulled her chair closer, making a loud screeching noise that made almost everyone in the coffee shop look over at her.

Adam made room for her to get closer to the screen. "You really don't know anything about your own game, do you?"

Demi gave him another shot to the arm. It was her way of showing affection toward him.

"That's Eve. Her world in Worlds is ranked number three behind you and me. She's also the CEO of a company called Interravision, which uses technology to try and make the world a better place. We've become really good friends over the past year. She's super talented."

"And super pretty."

"Yeah, I guess so."

There was an awkward pause for a moment as they both seemed to be examining Eve's photo on the screen.

"So is this the surprise?

Then, the bells on the door to the coffee shop

jingled, and Eve walked through the door.
"No, that's the surprise."

01000100 01100001 01110010 01101011 00100000 01001101 01100001 01110100 01110100 01100101 01110010

Demi immediately recoiled into her shell and became nervous about meeting someone new. She sank back into her chair, picking at her eyebrow as Adam stood up and waved for Eve to come join them. He pressed a button on the screen, and Eve's bio disappeared. They hugged for a little longer than normal in Demi's opinion, but she didn't know much about social norms.

After their hug, Eve looked at Demi and put her hands up to her mouth. "Is this ...?" She looked back at Adam, and he nodded his head. "Oh. My. God!" Eve pushed Adam aside and extended her hand out to Demi. She reluctantly placed her hand in Eve's and was pulled out of her chair, finding herself in a deep hug that made the one with Adam look like a pat on the shoulder. "Your game is unbelievable! I haven't stopped playing since you released it two years ago."

"Well, you're not playing right now, so I guess you had to stop at some point today." Even though Demi was being serious, both Eve and Adam laughed at what they thought was a sarcastic comment.

"And you're funny, too! I can't take this. Sorry, I'm fangirling so much. I'm embarrassing myself, aren't I?" She sat down on the opposite side of the table from Demi and Adam.

"No, you're fine, Eve. I was just telling Demi about how your World is ranked third. The top three all at one table. Pretty cool, right?"

They both stared at Demi waiting for a response.

"I've never really been concerned with the rankings. I just want to have my world and share the tech with others to maybe help them escape from the boredom of our reality."

"That's amazing." Eve quickly pulled up her screen, placed her drink order, and the drink took its tiny elevator ride through the hole in the table within seconds. "I was one of the first people to sign up for your game. When Adam told me about it and how you were going to release it to the world, I just knew I had to get my hands on it. Not only do you have an amazing game, but the tech behind the game is next level. I have so many questions for you but don't know where to start."

"Why don't you tell her about what's going on with the game, Demi?"

"Seriously, Adam?" She leaned over and whispered, "It was hard for me to even tell you about that, and now you want me to tell a complete stranger?"

"I think she can help," he whispered back and tilted his head toward Eve to encourage her to keep the conversation going. "Eve. Why don't you tell her about your company?"

"I get the sense that you're feeling a little

caught off guard."

Demi sipped her mint tea. "Yeah. A little."

"I'm going to cut straight to the point. I want to buy your game. My company, Interravision, is on a mission to help make the world a better place. We have a vision to utilize a wide range of different technologies, including artificial intelligence, to create a Utopia. The perfect world. We've been working with the government to simulate how we can get from our current state to a Utopian state, and I think your game is the key."

"Who would want to live in a perfect world, anyway?" Demi picked at her eyebrow.

They both looked at Demi with surprise as the conversation came to a complete halt. Eve powered through the silence and addressed the question presented.

"Imagine a world without crime, murder, stealing. Unlimited resources. Perfect harmony on our little ball floating through space."

"Sounds boring to me. We need the darkness to make the light mean more. You can't appreciate what you can see until the darkness takes the light away from you. We all want the things we *can't* have." Demi looked over at Adam for two reasons. One, to look for reassurance from him that she could speak her mind and not ruin his planned meeting—or whatever this was. And two, because she thought she couldn't have him, especially now that he's seen her in person.

"You know what? I agree." Eve sipped her

drink in an effort to prepare herself for another speech. "There may always be darkness in the world. But isn't it worth trying to rid ourselves of that darkness to help create a better world? Isn't that noble?"

"That's just the ego coming to the surface making you think you have the ability to change the world. You can only control what's right in front of you. But let's say you're able to achieve this Utopian society. What if someone just snaps one day and murders their neighbor? Animal instincts take over because some gene from their ancestors genetically pushes them to use the violence that's been passed down by generations upon generations."

"We're actually working on a project where we can splice DNA and control certain markers that potentially lead to negative behaviors around health and behavior."

"Now you're talking about playing God." Demi sipped her drink, accidentally mimicking Eve. "Look, it was great to meet you. I really am glad you like Worlds. Truthfully. But I have a lot on my plate right now, and I'm not ready to sell my game."

As Demi stood up to leave, Adam grabbed her hand. "Wait. Please."

"You'll have complete control over your world, Demi. You keep every morsel of that code, and I'll even keep your portion of the game on a separate server. It will all still be yours. Fully paid for and functional for as long as I live and breathe. I love this game, Demi. I would never want to take it away from you, and I don't want you to lose it either."

Demi sat back down and looked at Adam with her eyes piercing his. "You told her. Didn't you?"

"I'm only trying to help. I love this game too. I don't want to see it die because of a stupid thing like money."

"How does this sound to you?" Eve started scribbling on her napkin and pushed it over to Demi. She picked it up and looked at the nine-digit number with the dollar sign in front of it and almost fell out of her chair. She didn't pine for money like most people. The appeal came from having the independence to live in the world she created. To not have to worry about anything else in her actual world and have a sole focus on her digital world. This napkin held the key to everything she had ever dreamed of for herself.

"I keep my world?" Demi continued to stare at the napkin.

"Yes."

"You can't touch it?"

"Nope."

"What if your company goes bankrupt, or if you're bought out by another company in the future?"

"You still keep it."

"You said it will still be mine as long as you're alive. What if you die?"

"Everything tied to your world on this separate server would be turned over to you. Not only can I not touch your world, but no one else can either."

"I think you're going on a fool's errand."

"Maybe. But I'm willing to try."

They all sat in silence for a minute while Demi continued to look at the napkin. Then one last question popped into her head. "Why do you want to do this? Why do you want to turn our world into a Utopia."

"Honestly?" Eve sipped her drink again. "I had a son. He was everything to me. His father knocked me up and left me when he found out I was pregnant. He wanted to have an abortion, and I wanted to keep the baby. It was a struggle being a single mother and having a career at the same time. I ended up hiring a nanny to help. She was amazing and so great with Seth, but then, one day it all changed. She took Seth to the store and lost track of him. The police looked for weeks ... months to try to find him. Security footage showed him walking out of the store with a man, but they couldn't identify him. I kissed my baby that morning for the last time before heading out to work." Demi could tell Eve was holding back tears. "I would do *anything* to try to make this world a better place and get rid of someone who would kidnap a small child and take them away from their mom like that."

Feeling abandoned after the death of her parents, Demi understood the sinking feeling of what it felt like to lose someone you love. She felt heartbroken for Eve. A tear rolled down her cheek, and she quickly swiped it away.

"I may not agree with you on your Utopia, but I will admit ... what you're trying to do is noble. I'll sell you the game." Demi stood up and extended her hand to Eve. They shook on the deal, and they both smiled at each other.

Demi abandoned her cup of mint tea as she turned toward the door and walked out. Adam quickly said bye to a wide-grinning Eve and ran after her.

At the next block, he finally caught up to Demi. "Where are you going?"

She continued to walk, not making eye contact with him. "Home."

"Why are you so mad? I can't believe that just happened! I mean, you're gonna keep your world and everything will be paid for. You're set for life, Demi!"

Demi abruptly stopped in her tracks, planted her feet, and glared into Adam's eyes. "I didn't appreciate you telling her about what was going on with Worlds before I even had a chance to meet her. She obviously knew I was broke. Do you know how embarrassing that was for me? No, probably not. Because you're never embarrassed about anything."

"That's not true," he said with a warmth to it.

Demi looked away and folded her arms in front of her chest as she let out a deep exhale.

"Look, I'm sorry, okay?" He grabbed her hand, and Demi knew that had been the third time he had done that today. "You're totally right. I shouldn't have done that. I should have told you we were meeting her. I just didn't think you'd do it if I told you. You can be mad at me all you want if it means I helped you save your world. Because honestly ... you saved mine. I was so lost in this world before I found you. And I don't want to lose you now that you're here."

Demi glanced back at Adam from the side of her eye.

"Then tell me a time when you were embarrassed."

"Right now."

"Yeah."

"No, no. I'm embarrassed *right now*."

"Huh? Why?"

"Because I'm finally seeing you in person for the first time, and I can't work up the nerve to tell you how I feel about you. How you make my heart skip a beat every time you log on to Worlds and that sound plays through my headphones letting me know you're there. How your mind works like no one else I've ever met. How you scrunch your nose and flare out your nostrils when you're mad at something. I love everything about you."

The word "love" lingered in the air. Demi stood motionless. He stepped forward, put his lips an inch away from hers, and waited for her to make the final move.

She did.

01000100 01100001 01110010 01101011 00100000 01001101 01100001 01110100 01110100 01100101 01110010

All in one day, Demi found a way to keep her world alive and also managed to fall deeply in love with her best friend. It had been five years since that day, and she now sat on her front porch, watching her husband Adam play with their daughter Mary who was named after Demi's mom. They didn't have a white-picket fence, but it definitely felt like they matched the stereotype. Demi thought all she ever wanted was her own little world, but now, she had created her own little world in *real* life. A bubble only they could penetrate and a somewhat perfect reality if there ever was such a thing.

It felt nice being away from the city. The fresh air and the luscious fields filled with fruits, vegetables, plants, and flowers created a pallet of colors gleaming as far as Demi could see. She saw Adam pointing to the clouds, trying to show Mary something above. He told her how creative the clouds can be even though they aren't living things —they create their own shapes and patterns.

"Look, that one there. What do you see?" he asked Mary.

"A dinosaur!"

"I actually think it looks more like a shark, but now that you mention it ..."

Adam started to make dinosaur noises and

playfully tackled Mary into the grass.

Their smiles were infectious, and Demi's cheeks began to hurt from smiling so much watching the two loves of her life be silly together. A ding from her watch broke her out of her trance as she glanced at the notification. It was an automated alert to let her know a major event had taken place in her world.

"I'll be right back," she yelled down the steps to her family.

The front door of the house recognized it was Demi, and it automatically opened for her. The same happened when she turned the corner and approached the door to her study. A wide-angled holographic image of Demi's world popped up. A bright blue and green ball spun around and came to a stop.

The general greeting every time you log on to Worlds popped onto the screen, "Welcome to Earth!"

Demi walked up to her control panel and began sliding her fingers across the board to accomplish several tasks within only a few seconds. She had her settings programmed to where most of what needed to be done could be accomplished by only a few easy swipes and strokes of her finger.

A big, red bubble appeared in the top right corner stating, "Nuclear Attack Imminent!"

She swiped the notification away and saw a missile floating across the sky of her world. Pinching her fingers away from each other, she zoomed into the rocket-propelled missile and collected the data. It was projected to hit one of the newer countries Demi had developed—the United States of America.

"What are you going to do?" Adam stood in the door frame to Demi's office.

"I dunno, Adam. I knew this was coming, and I've thought about it a lot. This is what the people want. I gave them free will and look where it's taken them."

"Yeah, but you have a choice. You can save them. Maybe things will be different after."

If this nuclear missile continued on its path, it would create a nuclear war she knew would eventually wipe out her entire world and turn it into a dark cloud of dust floating through the Worlds' universe. It would be a relic for future gamers to visit. The original world created by the game's creator turned into a floating ball of dust as a reminder we are all headed on a path of destruction and non-existence.

However, she could divert the missile, or find some other way to not have it destroy her world. It was all up to her. She had less than one minute to decide if she wanted to save Earth or turn it into a nuclear wasteland.

"Reminds me of the dinosaurs." Adam was now standing next to Demi and latched on to her hand.

"Yeah, but that was a cop-out. I got bored and hit the restart button basically. This time it's *their* decision. No matter how much I love this world, it's theirs. They should be able to determine their future."

Adam didn't say a word and only stood by the woman he loved, supporting her.

"Sometimes the best decision we can make is not making a decision at all. Let it be as it may." Demi removed her hands from the console and took a step back.

Thoughts spun in her head as the timer began to tick away and tears filled her eyes. Less than ten seconds until impact. She watched as the time melted away to zero, and a bright light flashed across the holographic screen. It blinded Demi and Adam to the point they had to turn away and shield their eyes. Fire spread across the Earth as more missiles were launched. An apocalyptic fireworks show. She watched, knowing this was the end of the pretend world she had created, as mixed tears of sadness and joy spilled from her eyes.

Demi glanced down at Adam's hand holding hers. They both looked out the office window at Mary holding a flower in her hand and smelling it with a closed-mouth grin. Demi had a new life now with a daughter who needed every last morsel of her love and affection. Now wasn't a time for her to be living in some alternate reality playing games. She had a family to care for and create memories with. Earth would be her past, and she couldn't wait for her future in the real world. It may not be perfect, but to Demi, it sure felt like it was.

THE RENTAL

The Rental

I'll have Harold kill those rotten teenagers in the cabin in the woods!

This was the thought that came to James Davis' mind before he ended up scrolling a list of rentals looking for a getaway to finish his book. He had hit a case of writer's block, and he had finally broken through. Now all he needed was a secluded place to knock out this book and get his publisher off his back. This was the answer. This was how he'd end his book.

Writing was one of the hardest things a person could do, yet it was so simple. Sitting down one-on-one with the computer, clicking away—or at least trying to—seemed like an easy task, but the more you tried the further you fell away from it. "Just write," his publisher had told him. One of the best ways to get over this so-called writer's block was to change your environment. Find a place that was inspiring. And let's face it, he needed a change.

For James, writing had always come easy. The pages flowed like the Nile—but he was *stuck* right in the middle of this one with no way out. He's had a lucky career so far as a published author of two best sellers, and he knew he had a third on his hands if he could only get the words down on paper. The novel he was working on made its way into James' brain and couldn't fully make its way out onto the page. It seemed like there was a *force* holding him back. But now, he felt ready to roll.

James found a nice rental in the mountains in Western Maryland to help get his mind wired right. The place was perfect—right next to the water, and according to the map, there was only one other house nearby. He would have an office desk to work on and a wall full of novels in case he needed some time away from writing. He had a strong feeling this was the one. This was the cabin where he'd finish his novel, just like his main character would finish off those bastard kids in the cabin in the woods in his book.

He didn't have to ask his wife for permission to go on his writing retreat because they had been recently divorced. The trouble they ran into trying to make a baby became too much of a burden on their relationship. An unsuccessful marriage and the children that could have been nestled in the back of his brain buried beneath a mountain of anger and resentment. And now on top of it, he couldn't even write a simple story. Getting away from the city and secluding himself from the world seemed like the best idea for a fall week, especially now that he had the key to the conclusion of the story.

The three-hour drive was an easy one. The evergreens, pines, and different shades of yellow, red, and orange leaves had made James feel like he was driving through one of those landscape paintings you'd find in a hotel room. The ride had been enjoyable. He even had the windows down for the majority of the ride as he puffed on his Marlboro's—a new habit he'd rekindled since the divorce. Despite it being October, the weather felt more like a breezy spring day.

He turned off the main highway at the exit for the cabin and stopped at the gas station to fill up on more than just gas. He needed fuel for his writing retreat. Coffee, chips, Sour Patch Kids, and microwavable meals would do the trick. He walked past the alcohol aisle feeling his mouth water but decided against it. He'd gone a bit overboard with drinking since the divorce, and he had work to do this weekend. The gray-haired cashier with glasses as dense as the morning fog looked down at the pile of random items on the counter and then back up at James. "Where ya headin'?"

"Going out to a cabin a few miles up the road to get some writing done."

"Oh, you're a writer?"

James hated talking about his writing,

especially with strangers. He was worried talking about it might let the story seep out of his brain before he had a chance to get it on paper. At the same time, he didn't want to be rude to a nice, old man. "Yes, sir."

"What are ya writing about?"

"Not to answer your question with a question, but do you have a daughter?"

"Yes, sir. She's all grown up with kids now."

"Now what would you do if you found out a group of teenagers was bullying her in high school? What if one of them tried to sexually assault her?"

"I'd kill that sonuvabitch is what I'd do!"

"That's what my book's about."

"Interesting." James could tell the man was only being polite. "I haven't read in years. My eyesight's gone to shit since I hit 60. And hell, that was over a decade ago."

"Have you tried audiobooks?"

"Actually, no. But that's a great idea, son. You got any a those I could read ... err, I mean listen to? I like mysteries. The Hardy Boys were always my favorite."

"Look up *Smoke In Mirrors* by James Davis." And just like that, James had made a potential sale.

The cashier packed the snacks into plastic bags. "Will do and thank you for your business."

"Have a great day." James grabbed the bags and headed for the door.

"Hey, wait a sec." The cashier held out two packs of smokes. "You forgot these."

When James went to grab the Marlboro's, the cashier gave him a hard stare and asked, "Did you say you were heading up to a cabin?"

"Yeah..." James said hesitantly.

"Down yonder?" The cashier pointed west. "The one on Mulberry?"

For a moment, James thought maybe this guy might have the gall to follow him or try to pay him a visit at some point during the week to steal his car or any of his belongings. Being a writer of murder and mystery made everyone a suspect, even in real life. This gray-haired man seemed friendly enough and probably couldn't harm a squirrel in his elder state, or even see one through his thick glasses.

"Yes, sir. Right up on the lake."

"Alright, well, you be careful now."

James nodded and went to leave again, but the cashier's comment lingered. "What should I be careful about?"

"Well now, I'm not one to spread rumors or talk ill of others, but that place isn't ... right. Pretty much a mystery around here."

"Okay..." James waited for more detail, and his interest was piqued. Maybe he could use this "mystery" in his story somehow.

"The couple that lives in the main cabin are the Carson's. I only know their last name 'cause they rarely ever leave their house 'cept to go to the doctors or get essentials at the market, and that's how erryone refers to 'em anyhow. They never talk to folks and always pay in cash. Kind a strange for a small town if ya ask me. There've been a few ... I guess you could call 'em *accidents* up at their rental. The Sheriff has had to make a few trips up there in the past year. One guy went missing, and they never found him. Had his picture posted up all around town even. Then, a child went missing a few months back. Ended up at the bottom of Deep Creek Lake."

James stood with the bags in his hands, trying to decide how full of it this guy was, but part of him also thought it might be true. He continued to stare at the cashier blankly.

"Ah look, fella. I ain't tryin' to scare you or nothin'. I'm sure you'll be just fine. Thought you might like to know what you're getting yourself into is all."

"It's alright. Take care." James leaned his back against the door to push his way out of the store as quickly as he could and got into his car. He packed the smokes and pulled one out for his final leg of the trip to the cabin. The tobacco calmed his nerves as he drove slowly with the window down. The strange story about the Carson's and their rental reminded him of the start of a cheap horror flick, and it made him chuckle.

I'm sure they're fine people, he thought to himself as he turned onto Mulberry Lane.

01000100 01100001 01110010 01101011 00100000 01001101 01100001 01110100 01110100 01100101 01110010

James flicked his cigarette out the window just as he flicked away the thought of staying at a haunted cabin owned by the crazies in town. People in small towns tended to over-exaggerate things and bend the truth when it came to other folks. *Gossip makes the world go 'round*, he thought. The reviews on the rental were all great except for a few one-stars, but that's always the case with anything that can get a review—someone has to complain about something at some point. He knew that all too well with some of the negative reviews his books received online.

The trees on either side of Mulberry Lane swayed in the wind, creating a wave of leaves pulling James toward the cabin with its current. The sun slipped behind a stream of clouds as a darkening shadow grew over the property, and it felt as though the lines of trees on either side of the road were curling inward to swallow his car whole. As James rolled up his window, he noticed an old couple walking down the steps of the cabin, both holding cleaning gear—a mop, broom, rags, and other cleaning supplies. They both waved enthusiastically as they set their supplies into a small pull cart in the driveway. James' tires pushed into the gravel making a grating sound as he parked the car.

"G'mornin'!" the old couple yelled out at the

same time, as if they had practiced the greeting before.

"Morning." James walked up to the couple with his arm extended and shook both of their hands. He wasn't a tall man, but he still had to look down on the short couple who reminded him of hobbits without the furry feet. "James Davis. Nice to meet you both."

"I'm Rita Carson, and this is my husband Earl. We just got done cleanin' up in there for ya—not that it was dirty before. We like to keep the place spic and span, and we hope to keep it that way if ya catch my drift."

James now knew their first names and was reassured the old cashier was full of shit. The Carson's seemed like normal, down-to-earth people. He wasn't planning on throwing a big party at the cabin but understood the importance of someone wanting to take care of their property. "I'll treat it like it was my own, ma'am."

Rita peered through her thick spectacles across her wrinkly nose, somewhat frowning at the notion of being called "ma'am."

"Why don't you go on up and get lunch started for us, honey? I'll grab the cart." Then turning back to James, "Would ya like to join us?"

"I'm alright. Thank you." James lifted up his plastic bag of snacks.

Rita waddled across the grass toward the larger cabin that sat about a hundred yards away from the rental. "Enjoy your stay, Mr. Davis," she called out.

James waved to her as she turned away.

"So, what brings you to town anyways?" Earl spat and a brown liquid pooled on the ground.

"I'm an author. Looking for a quiet place to get some writing done." James stepped back to his car to open the trunk and pull out his suitcase.

"Oh, ya don't say. I never met a writer before."

"Yeah, we come out into the real world every now and then." James' joke seemed to fall on deaf ears as Earl stood stone-faced.

"I don't really read too much myself. We got a whole shelf full a books in the house, but it's all that crap Rita likes to read. What kinda books you write?"

Once again, James found himself discussing his work when he didn't want to. "Murder mystery mainly. I've only published a few books, but they're doing pretty well."

"That's not really up my alley. I read mostly non-fiction about the wars."

"Plenty of murder in those books, too."

He stared blankly at James with the same stone-cold expression and spat on the ground again.

"Well, hey. Thanks for cleaning the house up for me."

"Welcome." Earl held out a set of keys. "Enjoy your stay, Mr. Davis."

James grabbed the keys and lugged his suitcase up the stairs. When he got to the door to unlock it,

Earl was standing in the yard about halfway between the two houses staring at James until he went into the house.

01000100 01100001 01110010 01101011 00100000 01001101 01100001 01110100 01110100 01100101 01110010

A rustic smell coupled with Clorox made its way into James' nose. The floor creaked noisily as he walked through the surprisingly spacious cabin. A large family room area lined with wood all along the walls had two large windows facing the lake behind the house. He walked down the hallway to check out the bathroom and two bedrooms—one small room with two twin beds and a larger bedroom with a king bed and a private bath. He set down his suitcase and tested out the king mattress. Firm with some give, just the way he liked it.

Suddenly, a wave of exhaustion flooded his body. The bed was surprisingly comfortable. Being in a cabin in the middle of nowhere, it sure felt like he was lying on a bed in the Four Seasons downtown. Nothing wrong with getting a little rest and relaxation before he got down to business. He closed his eyes for a moment.

Beep!

His eyes opened, and he thought for a second his brain might be playing tricks on him.

Beep!

This continued for a few minutes until it was evident James wasn't going to get any rest before his writing stint. The green light from the smoke detector in his room glared at him. He stood up from his bed and looked directly up at the detector, waiting for it to beep again.

Beep!

That wasn't this detector beeping. There had to be another one in the house somewhere in need of a battery change. He went from room to room trying to locate the noise in a cat-and-mouse game of beep and seek. He could feel the beeping starting to irritate his brain. There wouldn't be any writing, let alone sleep, if the beeping continued. Finally, he found the culprit after identifying every smoke detector in the house. The red light on the one in the kitchen blinked every few seconds, indicating it had low battery. The only things to be found in the drawers of the kitchen were utensils and other small items one might find in a junk drawer, but no batteries.

James made the hundred-yard trek up to the Carson's main house and found Earl digging around in the back of his open garage.

"Hey there, Mr. Carson."

"Holy Christ, son. You scared the devil outta me." He had a scowl on his face as if someone had interrupted him from a nice steak dinner. "And call me Earl. Mr. Carson was my daddy."

"I'm sorry, Earl. I didn't mean to—"

"What can I help you with?"

"Sorry to be a pain off the bat, but one of the smoke detectors in the house keeps beeping. I looked for some batteries but couldn't find any. I won't be able to get any writing done with that beeping going on."

"Oh well, we wouldn't want that now would we?" Earl rubbed his hands into a shammy cloth and glared at James. All the kindness he had shown earlier seemed to have worn off as he seemed more than irritated. "I'm guessin' you want me to fix it, huh? Can't handle a little beeping." He puffed out an exhale as he pulled out a drawer in his toolbox.

"Well, yeah. I do appreciate it." James noticed a gun case in the corner of the garage holding multiple firearms. He figured that was about right considering he was deep into the country. Probably came with the house. "You do a lot of hunting?"

Earl grabbed a couple of double A batteries and turned to James who was looking at the gun case. "You could say that."

"I've never been. Don't think I'd have the guts to kill something. Unless it was in self-defense of course."

"Ain't that what most killin's about?"

"What do you mean?"

"Survival, son. A man who kills something only does so for his own benefit. And sometimes the best defense is a good offense. Catch my drift?"

James wasn't so sure he did, but he agreed quickly, looking to change the subject. "Want me to carry the ladder over there?" He put his hand on a painter's ladder leaning up against the wall near the garage door.

"Don't touch that!" Earl's voice boomed out of the garage and echoed in the surrounding woods of the property. "I mean … I got it, son. You're a guest here, and you shouldn't be doin' no labor. Sorry for shoutin'." His wide grin made him look like Jack Nicholson in that one scene when he played the Joker and didn't have any makeup. All the pleasantries the Carson's had offered him now seemed fake.

The door into the house opened, and Mrs. Carson poked her head through the frame. "Everything alright out here?"

"Dang smoke detector needs new batteries. You got lunch almost ready? I'm hungrier than a hippo in a board game."

"Keep your boots on, Earl. I just got done squeezin' the lemons. Sandwiches will be ready in a few." Then, turning to James, "You sure you don't want to have lunch with us, dear? Homemade lemonade is just as good in the fall as it is in the dead a summer. I got turkey sandwiches to go with it, and we got all the fixins."

"I don't want to be a bother." James looked at Earl when making this comment. At this point, he knew Earl had a temper and only wanted him to fix the "dang smoke detector."

Earl put on that fake smile. "Nonsense. You go on in and get yourself some grub while I head next door and fix that detector for ya."

Staying back with Mrs. Carson seemed like a more pleasant option than helping Mr. Carson with the smoke detector. Earl even gave him a gentle shove to guide him to the door that led into the house as he went to grab the ladder. James thanked them both and walked into the dampness of the Carson's home.

A black cat scurried past the laundry room door in a fret of terror seeing a stranger in the house. The smell of kitty litter and stale cat piss filled his nostrils as he walked through the laundry room and into the kitchen. There were stacks and stacks of newspapers surrounding the kitchen table. Mrs. Carson removed a smaller stack on the kitchen table and asked James to have a seat. There were knickknacks and other paraphernalia all around the house from what James could see from his seat at the kitchen table, including an absurd amount of roosters. All kinds of roosters. They were on the kitchen towels, a ceramic one on the counter, and they were even on the wallpaper. James thought, *Mrs. Carson must really love cock,* and chuckled under his breath.

An open cupboard with different-sized slots hanging on the wall had collected random items and reminded him of something his mother had as a child. There was a rusty key, a small fork that looked like a collectible of some sort, a small toy lifesaver, and a mini teapot to name a few of the items. James could have spent days, maybe even weeks, rummaging through all the junk his hoarding lunch mates kept in their house.

Mrs. Carson set a tall glass of lemonade on the table, startling James from his deficit of attention. "There ya go! Best homemade lemonade south of the Mason Dixon."

James took a sip. "Wow. You weren't kidding. That's really good." He took another big gulp.

"Thank ya, dear. Sandwiches comin' right up."

James glanced over at the stacks of newspapers, skimming some of the headlines.

AMERICA AT WAR! — HIKER STILL MISSING AFTER WEEK-LONG SEARCH — MARKET SEES BIGGEST LOSS IN A DECADE — MISSING CHILD FOUND IN DEEP CREEK LAKE

James looked over the stack of papers at the water behind the house. "That's Deep Creek Lake out there, right?"

"Sure is. One of the finest bodies of water in Maryland. You lookin' to get out there this weekend?"

"No, not really. I have a lot of writing to do." He sipped his lemonade and looked back at the headline in the paper—*Missing Child Found in Deep Creek Lake.* "Mrs. Carson. Can I ask you a question? And I hope you won't take offense."

She set a plate filled with potato chips surrounding a turkey sandwich cut in half diagonally in front of James and sat down next to him.

"Rita."

"Huh?" James pulled himself out of the trance the water from the lake had set upon him.

"Call me Rita, please." Her eyes fixed on James' and wouldn't let them go. For whatever reason, she seemed as peculiar about being called by her first name as Earl.

"Thanks for the sandwich ... Rita." He took a small bite and made an audible sound of enjoyment.

"What's your question?"

"Oh, right. I don't tend to be drawn into rumors or anything like that. But I heard you all have had quite a few accidents around here lately. Any truth behind that?"

Rita waved her hands in the air like she was shooing a fly away. "That's a bunch a nonsense if ya ask me. Bad stuff happens 'round here just like any other town. Even the ones that think they're so spic and span ain't got a perfect track record."

"What about the kid who was found in the lake?" He glanced over at the newspaper sitting on top of the stack. He could have sworn Rita made a face of disgust as if she was thinking out loud, *Why in the hell did I leave that article in plain sight*?

"Well, yeah. That's true." Rita stood up and walked back to the kitchen counter to fix Earl's sandwich for when he got back. "But nothing happened here at the house. That young boy was down at the public beach area and went missing. Found his body in the lake a few days later and figured he wandered out into the water and couldn't swim. They were staying in our rental, but like I said, nothing happened here at the house."

"Sounds like a freak accident."

"Exactly! It was a *freak* accident. Just like the man who had the heart attack."

"Someone had a heart attack in the rental?"

"Yes, sir. We went over to clean the house up and noticed his car was still in the drive. We went in and found him in bed dead as a door nail."

The door to the garage slammed closed, and Earl walked into the kitchen. "Goddammit, Rita! Why are you tellin' that story to our guest? He's trying to relax this weekend and get his writing done. Now you gone get him all upset."

"He was asking 'bout the ... uhh ... accidents."

"Don't believe a word she says. Too much true crime TV and mystery novels for this one." Earl grabbed his plate and sat next to James at the table. "I suppose you like all that though, considering you write about it."

"Yeah, I have a general interest in those types of stories. Helps me with my writing."

"I bet it does." Earl sat at the table across from James and took a monster bite out of his sandwich, chomping away at the bulging mesh of food stuffed into his cheek like a chipmunk.

Earl and Rita stared at James as he finished his sandwich like he was part of a science experiment, and he was their subject. Waiting for something to happen to him with each bite. He assumed they probably didn't get too many visitors in the main house, and from the sound of it, they weren't too sociable in the community. He scarfed down the remains of the sandwich and started to clean up his plate.

"Oh, don't you worry about that now. I got it." Rita picked up the plate and gave him a flirtatious grin as she turned back to the sink.

"Thank you for lunch," he called out to her and then turned to Earl. "And thank you for putting an end to that beeping. Would have driven me insane hearing that all weekend."

"Wouldn't want you to go crazy now, would we?" Earl's voice was sharp and seemed to cut through James' skin all the way to the bone. His friendlier tone from this morning seemed to have changed.

James thanked them once more as Rita escorted him to the front door. He looked back at her as he walked toward the rental, and she slowly waved her hand back and forth like the pendulum of a grandfather clock with a crooked smile. A smile that reminded him of the faces he imagined in his head as he developed evil characters in his writing. One that looked to be seeping through a mask.

James finally got some sleep and woke up with enough time to catch the end of the day and the setting sun over the lake. He rolled out of bed and thought he needed a cigarette and a snack before he got to his writing. He figured he might as well get on with it, or at least try, since that was the reason he was there in the first place. Writer's block be damned. He would put pen to paper that night—except he would really be clacking away on his keyboard.

He grabbed his laptop bag and sat at the desk in the family room. The view of the lake set him at ease as he loaded up his laptop. He grabbed one of the bags from the gas station and pulled out his smokes and a protein bar. After stuffing the bar into his face and taking a sip of water, the computer dinged, signaling it was ready for action. A nice shot of nicotine would help get his mind right before his writing session and give him a moment to collect his thoughts.

A loud ding came from the computer as he took the cigarette out and put it in his mouth to light up. The ding was an email from the rental company saying he had a message from the landlord of the property where he was staying. He wondered why the Carson's hadn't just come over to talk to him about whatever it was they needed and thought they probably didn't want to disturb him.

The message was short, clear, and in all caps.

"REMINDER: NO SMOKING INSIDE THE HOUSE!"

The cigarette in his mouth went from standing pointed in his lips to a dull hang in front of his chin. How could they know? James looked around the room, not really sure what he might be looking for. He stood up, went to the front window, and peered out, thinking he would see the shadows of the Carson's standing in the open grass between the two houses, but there was no one there. He walked to the back of the cabin and stepped out on the back deck. No one was there either.

The cigarette perked up in his lips, and he brought the Zippo lighter to it, puffing out a cloud of smoke and looking around the property inquisitively. The darkness was starting to creep in, and the sky turned to a dark purple as the red sun sat above the skyline, ready to dip behind the horizon. He looked across the backyard and didn't see the Carson's, although it was tough to see the back of their property through the line of evergreen trees.

He puffed on his cigarette, pacing back and forth on the deck, realizing he wasn't prepping himself for his writing session and was getting caught up in some nonsense he had swirling inside his head. He thought it was probably only a coincidence the email came through at that exact moment. One final drag of his smoke and he flicked the butt out into the yard. The red sun fell behind the horizon but continued to light up the sky with a purple hue that would eventually fade to black in a few minutes.

As he sat back into his chair, stretching, James noticed the smoke detector in the main room had a red light on it. He could have sworn it was green when he checked earlier. And if it was red, why wasn't it blinking or beeping like the one in the kitchen? He heard a loud creaking noise coming from the front porch. He glanced over and saw a shadow move across the blinds.

"Hey!" He pushed himself up from his seat and took a step back. "Who's out there? Rita? Earl?!"

He crept to the front door despite being freaked out and cracked it open a bit to see if anyone was on the porch. There wasn't a soul to be seen through the crack, so he opened it fully and took a cautious step through its frame. Looking around the property, he didn't see any sign of life, but he did see the porch light at the Carson's flick on. Only a few seconds later, the porch light on the rental turned on right behind him, which made James jump so hard it would have scared a flea off his scalp if he had one there. He caught his breath and figured it must be set on a timer or something.

He backed into the house, waiting for someone or something to jump out at him, but it turned out to be nothing. First, the weird email from the Carson's, and now this. Either someone was messing with him, or he was losing his mind. He thought it more likely to be the latter. Despite all the distractions, James opened his laptop and got to work.

01000100 01100001 01110010 01101011 00100000 01001101 01100001 01110100 01110100 01100101 01110010

Evidence Log: 485-A - Excerpt from *Daddy's Home* by James Davis

Chapter 26

"Open the door, you little shits!" Harold barked at the teenagers inside the cabin while he banged furiously on the door. "Nobody fucks with my daughter! Nobody!"

His voice was all of a sudden not his own. It scratched and clawed its way out of his throat like a demon from hell making its way to the surface. All reason and rational escaped him, and doctors would later state he had lost his mind. This was an entirely new person devoid of any normal human emotions. A true monster born of circumstance—a monster almost any father of a daughter would understand. While not every father would bring a sledgehammer to a teenage slumber party, they almost all would want some sort of revenge after finding out their daughter had been sexually assaulted, almost raped, and teased to the point of trying to commit suicide. In Harold's mind, he had almost lost his daughter, and there would be hell to pay. He was seeing red, and no one would get in his way.

The six teenagers sat huddled in the back of the family room, yelling at their phones to get service. Back in these deep woods, the cell phone towers were limited, and it would prove costly for these teenagers to be isolated from the outside world. For now, they were living in deranged-daddy hell.

"Fine! You wanna do this the hard way!?" Harold went to his car, opened the trunk, and pulled out his sledgehammer. He dropped the head of the hammer to the ground and dragged it across the rocks, making a grating sound as it made its way through the gravel driveway.

He thought the front door would be too obvious, so he casually walked around back, looking for another entrance to the cabin. Unfortunately for Blair, she also had a similar thought and tried to make a run for it at the behest of her five friends. As soon as she opened the back door and peered around the corner to see if the coast was clear, Harold pulled the sledgehammer back and took a hearty swing. The head of the hammer shattered through the door and crushed her head in an instant, sending wooden splinters, blood, skull, and bits of brain flying through the air.

Standing over Blair's now lifeless body with a devilish grin on his face, he tapped the remains of the back door with his sledgehammer and yelled out, "Daddy's home!" Knocking on the door again and again.

01000100 01100001 01110010 01101011 00100000 01001101 01100001 01110100 01110100 01100101 01110010

A knock at the door pulled James out of his zone. He was on fire and had written almost fifteen pages in less than an hour. The writer's block was finally gone, but somehow the distractions continued. This is exactly why he wanted to rent this house—to get away from all the distractions—and now someone was knocking on the fucking door. He sat for a moment wondering if he was only imagining it based on the timing with where he was at in his writing.

Another knock forced him to slam his laptop shut and head for the door. He slung it open, and Rita was standing on the porch with a slice of apple pie on a small paper plate.

"I'm so sorry to bother you, James. We had all this leftover pie, and I thought you might like a slice."

"Oh well, that's very kind of you." He grabbed the plate and smiled, but secretly he was yelling inside his head, *You goddamn bitch! You know I'm here trying to get some writing done and needed some peace and quiet, and you disturb me for a slice of fucking pie and ruin my flow.* "Thank you very much, Mrs. Carson."

"Rita." A scowl developed on her face as if she was able to read his mind. "Call me, Rita."

"Sorry, Rita." He cleared his throat. "Thank you for the pie."

"Have a good night." Her scowl turned to a smile, but to James, the smile felt forced.

"Same to you."

She turned away and slowly walked down the steps, putting both feet on each single step holding the rail with caution. Her old age definitely showed, and James thought about how awful it must feel to become old enough to where every bone in your body ached and simple movements like walking down the stairs would be a chore. Getting old wasn't for the weak-minded.

He closed the door and locked it, hoping there wouldn't be any more disturbances. Maybe he could get back in his seat, open his laptop, and pretend like this hadn't happened. He could revert right back into his flow state. A sudden realization hit him—why didn't he ask her about the perfectly timed email? He brushed it off as he set the pie on the desk.

About an hour later, the cursor on his screen blinked almost as if it was taunting him. Frustrated, he slammed his laptop shut and began eating the pie.

01000100 01100001 01110010 01101011 00100000 01001101 01100001 01110100 01110100 01100101 01110010

The muscles in his body felt weak, and he felt a rush to his head after taking the first drag of his cigarette on the back deck. His digital watch glowed onto his face as he read the time at quarter to midnight. Despite taking a nap earlier in the day, a wave of fatigue slammed into his body. James pinched his nose, rubbing the inside corners of his eyes. This damned writer's block was starting to take its toll on him, especially after getting in his flow state and then losing it. Recapping where he was in the story would sometimes help him get back on track in the past.

The group of kids were in the cabin playing drinking games. Harold was having his *Shining* moment, knocking on the cabin door. One of the girls tried to escape out the back door and boom. *Now what*? he thought. The scene was starting to get rolling in his head, but it still felt blank. This was Harold's moment. The part of the story where he snaps. The climax if you will. James was excited to get to this part—the "fun part" he called it. The scenes where the killer went off. This was his bread and butter, and the damned block wouldn't break. James slammed the butt of his cigarette on the handrail of the deck and flicked it out into the yard.

A rustle in the evergreens between the rental and the Carson's house caught the corner of his eye as he walked back into the cabin. He paused, keeping his eyes trained on the trees and didn't see anyone.

"Who's out there?"

No answer.

"I see you."

No response.

James didn't actually see anyone, and if

someone was in fact there, they called his bluff. It was probably an animal, but in his head, he felt the slightest suspicion that it was the same shadowy figure that had been on the front porch earlier that evening. He quickly jumped inside, shut the door, and locked it while scanning the backyard. No sign of life.

The combination of the writer's block, the sudden wave of fatigue, and the creepiness of the cabin started to wear on James. The headache quickly turned to a migraine and started to take shape in his temple. He could feel the vein starting to pulsate as he rubbed his forehead. He lay down on the couch and closed his eyes.

Beep!

"Seriously?" he said out loud.

Beep!

The red light on the smoke detector on the ceiling of the room was blinking.

James screamed out, "Son of a bitch!"

Then his phone dinged with an email notification. It was from the rental company again.

Beep!

He opened the email, and there was a short message.

"Thank you for not smoking in the house. Enjoy your stay!"

James' mouth opened, and a little drool almost fell out as his vision began to blur. "What the fuck?! Who in the hell is sending these messages?" He realized he was saying these things out loud as if he was talking to himself. Then he thought, *Am I going crazy?*

Beep!

This time he let out a disapproving grunt. He couldn't wake up the Carson's this late at night, but part of him wanted to bang on their door with all his might and make that grumpy old man climb up on his ladder again. The ceiling was too high for him to reach up and grab the smoke detector without a ladder. He'd have to problem-solve this one on his own somehow if he wanted the damned beeping to stop.

Beep!

Then, he noticed the owner's closet next to the kitchen and thought maybe there would be a ladder he could use ... or something. It was locked. He pulled one of the kitchen chairs out and stood on it, barely allowing him to reach the smoke detector. It twisted off with ease except it was caught on a wire. He tried to find the source of the wire to disconnect it, but it went through the ceiling. The wire finally disconnected on the other end closest to the smoke detector. He took the batteries out and threw them across the room as the last *Beep!* faded away.

Looking up at the now hanging wire coming through the ceiling, he noticed the tip of the wire was almost clear. He reached up to pull it closer to him, and it looked like a lens. *Is this a camera*, he thought?

Out of the corner of his eye, James saw another

shadow quickly move across the open windows in the front of the house, and he almost screamed as the chair he was standing on lost its balance, tipping him over. His head hit the ground, and his vision went black.

01000100 01100001 01110010 01101011 00100000 01001101 01100001 01110100 01110100 01100101 01110010

James woke up half an hour later with a migraine, but it felt more like two rhinos were banging into each side of his head. His vision managed to regain focus, and his eyes immediately became glued to the wire sticking out of the ceiling. Quickly realizing his situation and how he ended up passed out on the floor, he turned his head to the window where he saw the shadowy figure as if only a few seconds had passed since he fell.

He ran to the door and swung it open. Only the crickets and other nocturnal animals could be heard as they made an orchestra of late-night lake sounds in the distance. An owl hooted, and it locked eyes with James from across the drive at the edge of the woods. Its large wings made a swooping sound as it fell from a branch and caught the breeze of the wind, gusting away in a fury that was both frightening and exciting. A picture frame fell to the ground as he slammed the door shut, and an electronic dashboard was revealed.

The screen came to life as he touched it, asking for a password. A banner stretched across the top of the screen with the words "Simpson Security Systems" and a logo with three S's scrunched together.

"What in the actual fuck!? Are you watching me?" James knew they were watching, but he still asked the question out loud. While it was a rhetorical question, he still answered the question in his mind. *Yes*, he thought, *those old, creepy mother fuckers are spying on me.*

That's it, James' voice continued in his head. *I'm going over there right now to confront them.*

"I'm coming over *now*!" His voice echoed through the cabin.

Click!

He wasn't sure what the noise was, but it sounded like a door shutting down the hallway. Or it could have been the front door. He wasn't sure. The click had also echoed through the cabin, so it was hard for him to determine where the sound came from. He shook his head and yelled out, "You have some explaining to do!"

James twisted the knob on the door, but it didn't open. The door was locked. *But I just opened this up a few minutes ago*, he thought. *Was that where the clicking noise came from? Did they somehow lock the door using this Simpson app?* He doubted an old couple like that could manage a security system, let alone an app on a phone. I guess anyone who can make a turkey sandwich or change the batteries in a smoke detector could handle clicking a button on an app to lock a door.

Every door in the cabin was now locked. He even tried the windows, and those were locked too. He couldn't believe he was seriously locked inside this rental with no way out, and he was being spied on to top it all off.

"Open the door, you motherfuckers!" Despite his situation, there was still a sliver of doubt whispering in his ear that this was all in his head. He thought about calling 9-1-1, but that seemed extreme at this point. What would he tell the cops when they arrived? *Sorry to bother you at one in the morning, sir, but these old people locked me in their house, and they're spying on me.* He didn't even know if a rental owner could legally have cameras in the house or not.

The next instinct he had was to call his ex, Jennifer. She was a lawyer and would know what to do. Also, it was a good excuse to call her, especially when he wasn't shitfaced like every other time he had called her since their divorce.

"Hello?"

"Jenny! Oh, thank God!"

"It's the middle of the night, James. Why in the hell are you calling me so late? Or at all for that matter?" Her voice was low and calm like she was trying not to wake someone up, but he could still feel her anger through the phone.

"This isn't a joke, and no, I'm not drunk."

"Yeah, right. I bet you—"

"Seriously, Jenny! I'm not fucking around. I

need your help. I'm in trouble.

Her tone through the phone all of a sudden became warm and empathetic. "Okay, James. Calm down. What's going on?"

"Is it legal for an owner of a rental property to have security cameras in the house?"

"Can't you fucking Google that? Jesus."

In his head, he actually agreed with her. He could have Googled it, but then he wouldn't be talking to her and wouldn't hear her opinion on his situation.

"Jenny. Please."

"I think it's legal in most states. They can't put them in private areas like bedrooms and bathrooms. I'd check online though. What's this all about?"

"The landlords of this rental are fucking with me."

"How?"

"The smoke detectors are going off, I'm seeing shadowy figures in the windows, and they *fucking* locked me in the house, Jenny. I can't open any doors or windows. They've taken me hostage, and I just found a tiny camera in the smoke detector."

Jennifer let out a long groaning breath. "James. Listen to me. You have to stop doing this. You can't call me anymore. I have to tell you something."

James had a feeling he knew what she was about to say, and the pie turned over in his stomach.

"I'm getting married."

Those three words cut through his heart like a samurai sword slicing a watermelon. It seemed so easy for her to say them. They were so hard for him to take. The woman he loved with every part of his being was going to be with someone else. Forever. His situation in the cabin became an afterthought as every blood vessel traveled to his pulsating head with anger.

"It's only been six months since we divorced, Jenny. Are you for real?"

"If I'm being honest ... I've been with him for longer than six months."

"Are you FUCKING KIDDING ME!?!"

A beeping similar to the sound he heard from the smoke detectors was now coming from his phone after the call dropped. For a moment, he thought she hung up on him, but then soon realized he no longer had service. He rushed over to his laptop and saw there wasn't a Wi-Fi signal either.

James flipped the small wooden table over on his side and screamed. He picked up the chair and threw it at the glass door at the back of the house, but it bounced right off and back onto the floor, barely leaving a smudge. He tried again and again, but the glass wasn't normal glass. It was bulletproof and unbreakable.

His chest heaved up and down from exercising his anger, and the whites in his eyes were almost completely red with veins that they felt like they were pulsating from the back of his brain all the way around to his temple and now settling right behind his eyes.

The door to the owner's closet caught his eye.

"What the fuck are you hiding in there?" His voice echoed with his footsteps as he approached the door and wiggled the locked knob of the door.

"Open *fucking* sesame!"

01000100 01100001 01110010 01101011 00100000 01001101 01100001 01110100 01110100 01100101 01110010

Evidence Log: 482-C - Excerpt from *Daddy's Home* by James Davis

Chapter 4

"You know I would do anything for you, right, Lisa?"

"Yeah I know, Daddy."

"Do you want me to go down to the school and talk to the principal? This kind of stuff should not be happening on school grounds. Your mother is so upset." Harold thought it was strange he was the one with the level head in this situation. His baby girl had every right to be upset, and usually, Janice handled these types of situations—not that they occurred all the time, but Lisa was a little on the unusual side. They had always said she was "unique" or "special", but the other kids at school only saw her as weak and weird.

"Can you tell me again what happened,

sweetie?"

"I dunno. It's not that big of a deal."

Now, he knew she was lying. Everything to a freshman in high school was a big deal, especially when it came to friends and fitting in.

"It is a big deal. Let's talk this through, and maybe we can figure it out together. Like one of those mystery books we would read together."

"There's nothing to do, Daddy. Some of the kids at school were just teasing me. I'm fine."

Harold knew she didn't want to talk about it. It was embarrassing getting picked on at school. He knew all too well and thought maybe he could share his experiences to make her feel better.

"You know, I got picked on in school, too."

"You did?"

"Yeah."

"For real?"

"Yeah, I didn't hit my growth spurt until Junior year of high school. Freshman year was tough on your old man coming in only weighing about a buck twenty soaking wet. The older kids would push me around in the hallways, stuff me in lockers—all the typical hazing a dorky freshman like me tends to receive. But one time, Big Joe Harrington took it too far. He decided to pin me up against the wall in the bathroom for no apparent reason—probably because his daddy didn't love him enough. Big Joe was obviously ... well, big. While he pinned me up against the wall, he questioned if I had any balls, calling me girly

names and trying to attack my manhood. And then, he actually attacked my manhood and kneed me in the crotch. I fell to the ground, trying to catch my breath and waited for my balls to drop back down out of my stomach."

Lisa giggled at her dear, old dad using the word "balls."

"By the time I got my wits back, Joe was laughing at me with a few of his knucklehead friends. I felt a kind of rage in me I've only felt a few times in my entire life. I felt like I could have killed him, if I'm being honest with you. But instead, when he leaned down to call me another name, I came up with a right uppercut that sent him all the way to Sunday. I gained some credit that day with the rest of the school. I overheard one kid say, 'Did you hear Harry knocked out Big Joe?' He never messed with me again."

"Wow. So you stood up for yourself, and they backed off?"

"Yep! Now, I'm not saying that's what you need to do. We don't need you to go around school trying to knock people out. But I think it's important you know ..."

His pause made Lisa raise her posture. "What, Daddy? What is it?"

"The rage. We all have it. Every single one of us is born with the ability to lose it. That's the easy way out, though, hon. Yes, I want you to stand up for yourself, but you have to know how to control the rage before you use it, or else, you'll

be out of control."

"So don't fight back?"

"I'm not saying that. I trust you to make the right decisions, sweetie."

"Thanks, Daddy."

Harold wiped a tear from her cheek. "Besides, you have me. I'll do anything to protect you, Lisa. Anything."

01000100 01100001 01110010 01101011 00100000 01001101 01100001 01110100 01110100 01100101 01110010

Everything came piling up on top of James at that moment. The failed marriage, the child he would never father, the inability to finish his novel, and his ex-wife now soon to be re-married. He didn't have a family. He didn't have a purpose. Nobody cared about his writing. His desire to create a fictional daughter and protect her outweighed his need to write a compelling novel. And now his stupid decision to go to a secluded rental wasn't only backfiring on him, it was crawling under his skin, driving him mad.

He stood in the middle of the room with his eyes glued to the doorknob of the owner's closet as he swayed back and forth. The sound of his Zippo flicking on echoed in the room as he lit his cigarette. He tilted his head back and blew the smoke directly at the hidden camera poking out of the ceiling where the fire detector once was. Usually, cigarettes calmed James down, but now, they seemed to be igniting the rage inside of him.

His heart rate increased rapidly. The headache continued to pulse at his temples.

After taking several puffs, he dropped the cigarette on the floor and stomped it out with his boot. Looking up at the camera with his last puff, he yelled out, "Fuck you!" and walked over to the closet. His hand grasped the knob, and it turned unexpectedly. He thought it would be locked like it had been before, but somehow, it wasn't locked anymore. When he pulled the door open, he fumbled through several items you'd typically see in an owner's closet—paper towels, toilet paper, cleaning supplies, some tools, a bottle of moonshine, and a flashlight.

As soon as he picked up the flashlight, the electricity in the cabin shut off, and the humming from the HVAC system came to a halt, creating a deafening silence. James clicked on the flashlight and pointed it into the now-darkened closet. The light landed directly on a long wooden stick, and James moved the light down the handle, figuring it was a broom or something. But it wasn't. It was a sledgehammer.

01000100 01100001 01110010 01101011 00100000 01001101 01100001 01110100 01110100 01100101 01110010

As soon as James grabbed the handle of the sledgehammer, he felt the rage within him course through his blood. This was his way out. While his main character Harold used it in his story to clobber a mean girl's head through a door, James would use it to get through the door and out of this haunted cabin once and for all.

His first thought was to take it to the front door, and he pulled the sledgehammer over his shoulder and took a baseball swing at the panel next to the door that was now blank with no power in the house. The screen cracked, but nothing happened. He checked the door, and it was still locked. He took a swing at the door, and it didn't even make a dent. After using all his strength with several swings, there was barely a mark on the door. *It must be fortified somehow*, James thought, *just like when I tried to throw the chair through the window.*

Next, James tried wailing on the windows, and again, nothing happened. Barely a scratch. That was when he got really angry. When you cornered a rabid dog, he would try to fight his way out every single time, and that was how James felt. The need to fight his way out took over his body.

He swung that sledgehammer across the entire cabin, feeling as if the sledgehammer somehow had control over him. While it seemed the frame of the cabin wasn't budging, everything inside its walls was fair game. The sledgehammer tore through the kitchen, breaking almost every dish in sight. It put a hole through the oven and almost knocked the refrigerator door off its hinge. It made its way to the bedrooms and destroyed every piece of furniture he could find. Feathers and cotton flew through the air as he crushed his bed with the sledgehammer. The shelf of paperbacks was his last target, and it felt damn good to wreck all those completed novels.

"Fuck you and fuck this house, you motherfuckers!"

Red veins continued to fill the whites in his eyes, and he realized, there truly was no way out. He was almost out of breath from taking batting practice across the entire cabin. He took several deep breaths and was able to calm himself down a bit, although his adrenaline was still pumping. He remembered seeing the bottle of moonshine in the owner's closet and grabbed it. He dragged the sledgehammer across the floor with the now open bottle in his other hand as he took a few gulps.

He managed to find the one last piece of furniture that survived his onslaught—a kitchen chair lying sideways on the ground. He picked it up and sat in the chair, staring at the front door, thinking he could maybe force it open with his mind since the sledgehammer didn't work.

The pack of cigarettes crumpled in his pocket when he sat in the chair, and he pulled them out along with his phone. The time read 2:36 AM, and the battery went dead. Not that it mattered since he didn't have a signal to make a distress call to someone like his bitch ex-wife who didn't believe him. The same bitch who cheated on him and was about to re-marry less than six months after they divorced.

James lit the last cigarette he ever smoked and

continued staring at the front door as the Zippo continued to burn. After a few drags, he felt a wave of exhaustion hit him like a tsunami, but he still managed to take a hefty chug of the moonshine as it spilled out of the sides of his mouth and onto his clothes. After several chugs, he lost his grip on the bottle, and it came crashing to the ground with a shattered bang. The moonshine covered his entire body and pooled on the ground beneath him.

"Goodnight, James."

He heard the distant voice in the back of his mind, not sure who, or what, it was. It repeated the phrase over and over again, reminding James of when his mom would tuck him in and kiss him on the forehead. It was a smooth, calming voice like one you'd hear on a meditation app.

"Goodnight, James. Goodnight."

And with the final goodnight, James' head slumped down, touching his chin to his chest, and he was out cold. Once he started snoring, the burning cigarette in his hand fell to the ground along with his Zippo. The lit cigarette didn't mix well with the moonshine, and lighter fluid from the Zippo ignited a fire. Sweat started to bead on his forehead while he continued to sleep, and the flames grew. They made their way up his legs and onto his alcohol-drenched shirt, turning him into a torch within a matter of seconds.

James, the human fireball, began running around the cabin frantically and started banging on the glass of the back door, staring at the lake and hoping he could somehow make it there. With the house still on lockdown, there was no escape for him. He remembered to stop, drop, and roll, but all that seemed to do was spread the fire around the cabin even more. The bookshelf full of novels, now lying in a cluttered pile on the ground, caught fire. Every word on every page would burn into history just as the remaining words of *Daddy's Home* would be lost forever—trapped inside the melted mind of James Davis. Within a few short minutes, the cabin that had claimed several lives before James was now up in flames, on its way to ash like everything else in the world.

01000100 01100001 01110010 01101011 00100000 01001101 01100001 01110100 01110100 01100101 01110010

Earl Carson sat at his kitchen table, petting his black cat. The long, smooth strokes from the back of its head down to its tail not only made the cat purr, but it was also relaxing to Earl. Rita had just walked in from the antique store and started to unwrap an item buried in brown paper. She held up a small ceramic ornament of an old-school typewriter like the one Jack Torrance wrote, "All work and no play makes Jack a dull boy," over and over again. It fit the situation well enough, and Rita placed it in an empty slot next to the lifesaver and rusty key. These items were a way for the Carson's to honor those who had been taken by the cabin. A reminder that evil lived next door and could strike at any moment—well, not anymore, thanks to the fire.

"Perfect." Rita took a few steps back, admiring their collection.

"'Spose that will be the last of it."

"I sure hope so. You hungry? I can wrestle up some ham sandwiches."

"No, I'm fine."

They glanced down at the morning paper that had the headline in bold letters across the top:

LOCAL RENTAL BURNS TO THE GROUND; ONE GUEST DEAD

"Says it was an accident. I guess booze and cigarettes don't mix well." Earl pushed the paper over to Rita, and she sat to read. "We tried to warn him about smoking in the house. Wish we could a done more."

"Oh, honey, don't beat yourself up. We did everything we could. The damned house was haunted, and you know it."

"Yeah, well, now it's gone."

"The insurance money will be nice. Maybe we can finally take that cruise we've been talking 'bout."

"Yeah. Maybe."

Rita unfolded the paper to read more. After a few minutes of silence, while she read, she shook her head. "He was a nice boy. Says here he didn't have no family. I'd be feeling a hell of a lot more guilty if he left behind a wife and kids."

"Nobody cries for the lone soldier."

"Yeah, I guess not."

They sat in silence again for a few minutes while Rita looked out the window, and Earl made the black cat purr.

"At least we don't have to clean that damned house anymore." Earl let the cat down off his lap. "Go on, girl."

"That thing would have found a way to kill us if we didn't take care of it so well."

"Good idea making it a rental, hon. Kept that thing fed and off our backs."

"I wish we woulda thought about burning it down ourselves before we got all those people killed."

"Eh, I thought about it once. We woulda been taking a huge chance. What if the house didn't burn all the way down, or if it tried to retaliate? I coulda been a burnt hot dog like Mr. Davis. No, thank you."

"Well, I'm glad it's over."

After dipping her tongue in her water bowl, the Carson's black cat made its way outside. The charred remains from the burnt house created an aroma that smelled like the end of a campfire but much stronger. The cat slithered toward the cabin to investigate. Maybe there were some nicely cooked rats or mice for her to chew on.

As she approached the burned-down cabin, the cat suddenly crouched into the grass, feeling something was off. They say animals have a sixth sense that can detect certain things humans can't. In this case, she could feel the *force* still coming from where the cabin had stood, and she suddenly dashed away and up into a tree next to the Carson's house.

That cat would have been a nice little desert after the meal it had, but the force would have to suffice with its only meal that week—James Davis. It would remain there, ready to feed on its prey. Always ready for its next victim.

HAVEN

Haven

Dianne Reynolds knew this was the end. Not the end of a song she wanted to keep playing, or the end of a book she wanted to keep reading. This was the end of her life.

"I'm really sorry to break this news to you," the doctor began as he looked down at his tablet. "You have stage 4 pancreatic cancer. It's started to spread to other parts of the body. We've had some advancements to catch this early, but we're too late."

"I guess this is what I get for never going to the doctor." She took a deep breath. "How long?"

"Excuse me?" The doctor looked up from his tablet.

"How long do I have to live?"

"I'd say about three months. Maybe less."

Aside from the doctor tapping on his tablet, a heavy silence hung between them.

"Can I see my daughter now?"

"We've contacted her, and she's on her way."

All Dianne cared about was spending time with her family—her daughter Ella was married to the perfect son-in-law, and they gave her an amazing granddaughter, Belle. A small tear rolled down her cheek, not because she had just learned about her impending death, but the fact that she wouldn't see her Belle grow up. Most people see a vision of their past before they die—a video of the mind showing all their impactful memories. Not Dianne. Her vision was of the future and Bella's graduations, her wedding, her first job, and the great-grandkids she would never meet.

"There's a grief counselor waiting outside the door ready to chat with you if you'd like." The doctor tapped on his tablet furiously as he spoke. "News like this can be hard to take, and I want to make sure you have all the resources available to you." While the doctor seemed empathetic to Dianne's situation, he continued to look down at his tablet as if he'd said the same line to a hundred other patients already that day.

"After dozens of years of research, you still haven't come up with a cure yet?"

"I'm sorry, Mrs. Reynolds. There have been some advancements, but a cure is unlikely at this point. AI technology hasn't even been able to figure this one out for us."

She scoffed at his response grudgingly. "We've sent an entire colony to the moon, solved the climate crisis, ended world hunger, yet we're still unable to get rid of the big C."

"I'm truly sorry, Mrs. Reynolds." This time he looked up from the tablet. "We're going to do everything we can to make you as comfortable as possible. Would you like for me to send in the grief counselor?"

"No. I'm okay. I just want to see my daughter, Ella."

"We'll give her a call for you. Hang tight."

Dianne looked down at the wrinkles on her hands while the doctor left the room. All at once, the present moment hit her like a wave crashing down on the shore. She thought about her hands and if she'd paint with them again. Would everything she did from here on out be the last time she did that thing? There would be a last breath. A last bite of food. A last walk. A last sunset. One last time looking into her daughter's eyes. One last hug from her granddaughter. And one last sleep. The eternal sleep.

A small knock woke her from her meditation.

"I'm so sorry to bother you, ma'am." A young woman with a comforting face approached her bedside slowly. "I'm the grief counselor, and I—"

"I told the doctor I only wanted to see my daughter."

"That's okay, ma'am. I understand. I just wanted to leave these here with you if that's alright." She placed several pamphlets on the table next to Dianne's hospital bed. "Please don't hesitate to let the doctor know if you change your mind."

Dianne gave her a close-lipped smile and thanked her. She looked down at the stack of pamphlets laid out on the table like a deck of cards, and one of them caught her eye—the bright blue neon lettering made this pamphlet stick out from the rest, and at first glance, it looked like it said "Heaven" at the top. She picked up the pamphlet along with her reading glasses to investigate.

The big, neon blue word at the top of the pamphlet came into focus, and it said "Haven" and under that the subtitle read, "Your Paradise for Eternity." Dianne continued to read the entire pamphlet, unfolding it and soaking up every detail. As she read, the tears on her cheeks began to dry, and her saddened face grew a smile.

"My paradise for eternity," she mumbled to herself, leaning her head back against her pillow and looking up to the heavens. "That sounds amazing."

01000100 01100001 01110010 01101011 00100000 01001101 01100001 01110100 01110100 01100101 01110010

Belle crawled her way toward Dianne's feet as if she were a spider making her way to her prey, and she noticed she couldn't move. Her arms and legs were spread wide, and they were stuck to a large web. The heart rate monitor in the hospital room beeped faster and faster, and the sound grew louder and louder in her ears as the spider child approached. When it started to crawl up her legs its kaleidoscope eyes darted up at her. Fangs grew from its mouth as it opened, and it began to sink its teeth into her legs. She screamed out in agony as it sucked the blood out of her body. It began to spin her around and around, balling her up into a cocoon to prepare its feast. The room continued to spin until she stopped, and those beady eyes from the spider child pierced her soul. It leaned its head back and extended the fangs in its mouths, and as soon as it went in for the final kill, Dianne woke from her nightmare.

"Mom! It's me!" Ella grabbed her shoulders to hold her still. "I'm right here. Everything's okay."

Although, it wasn't—Dianne was on her deathbed. Well, maybe not just yet. But everything definitely wasn't okay.

She grabbed at her neck to see if she had spider bites at the point of attack, but there was nothing there. "I ... uhh ... I had a nightmare. Sorry, sweetie."

"It's okay. I'm here, Mom." Tears rolled down Ella's cheeks, knowing full well the gravity of why her mother was in a hospital bed.

Dianne reached out and held her daughter's hand in comfort. "Where's Belle?"

"She has school today. I can bring her by this evening if you'd like."

"Are they going to let me out of here soon? I hate hospitals. I don't want to be in here another minute."

"I know, Mom."

"I don't want to die in this damned hospital bed. That's for sure."

Ella's crying elevated at the thought of her mother's impending death. Tears continued to stream down her face, and she looked as if she had been crying for hours.

Dianne squeezed her hands. "It's alright, dear. It's only death."

"Mom ... I don't want to lose you. Is there a possibility you can make it out of this? They've made so many advancements in technology lately. There has to be a way to beat this. We need to talk to the doctor."

On cue, the doctor walked into the room continuing to look at his tablet with a nurse in tow.

"Good afternoon, Mrs. Reynolds." The nurse checked the monitor next to the bed and began typing furiously on the keyboard. "Are you ready for your lunch?"

"I'm not hungry." Her face had sunken in at the cheeks and hallowed out her eyes, stating the contrary.

"Mom, you need to eat."

The nurse came to the side of the bed, almost pushing Ella to the side. She shuffled her pillow and checked her IV. "You don't have to eat right now. It's okay, Mrs. Reynolds."

And once again, Dianne was brought to the realization that nothing was okay. The more everyone around her tried to say, "It's okay," the more she realized it wasn't. It's not that she was scared of dying. She only felt she had more time on this Earth. More time to cross out items on her bucket list. More time to watch her granddaughter grow.

The nurse squeezed Dianne's shoulder in comfort and walked out of the room as the doctor continued his checkup.

"How are we feeling after our nap, Mrs. Reynolds?"

"I'm fine. When can I go home?"

"I'd like for you to visit with an oncologist for further testing. Your chances of survival are slim, but there's still a possibility."

"Another doctor? I don't want to spend the end of my days in a waiting room."

"It's your choice, of course. But I highly encourage you to reconsider." He finally looked up from his tablet at Dianne and then turned his focus on Ella. "Are you able to care for your mother? You'll need the proper equipment if you're going to take her in, or we can look at hospice care."

"I'm *definitely* not spending the rest of my life in a home with a bunch of dying old people." She realized the irony of the statement fully knowing she was in fact a dying old person herself. Still, she clung to the idea she was younger with plenty of life in front of her.

The doctor looked back down at his tablet as if to find some way out of this conversation. Doctors aren't too thrilled when a patient doesn't want to take their expert opinion.

"We can take her in, doctor. Whatever we need to get. No matter the cost."

Dianne grabbed her daughter's hand again and squeezed. "Sweetie, no. I'm not going to put that burden on you."

"You'll get to spend more time with Belle, Mom. More time with me."

The doctor chimed in. "I'll give you both some privacy to discuss. The nurse will be back soon to check on you." He walked out of the room, looking down at his tablet, swiping at it.

Ella didn't want to discuss the topic anymore. She only wanted to hold her mother, so she leaned down and hugged her tightly. The pamphlets sitting on the table next to the bed caught her attention, especially the neon blue pamphlet.

"Haven? What's this?"

"I've made up my mind. This is the future of the afterlife, and I want to do it. I can't stay in the hospital, I don't want to go to a home, and I don't want to burden you and your family."

"I dunno, Mom. This is still in the testing phase. They've barely used it on humans at this point."

"What do I have to lose?"

01000100 01100001 01110010 01101011 00100000 01001101 01100001 01110100 01110100 01100101 01110010

"Welcome to Haven, Mrs. Reynolds. My name

is Peter, and I'll be providing you with a tour today."

The lobby of Haven's headquarters was breathtaking with glass ceilings three stories high, marble flooring, leather couches, and a snack bar free to all guests. For Ella, it brought some legitimacy to the company and blanketed her skepticism, but only for a moment. Peter escorted them past security as they walked through scanners that checked for any nefarious items. A security guard stopped them and asked to check Dianne's wheelchair. He padded the pocket on the back and used a mirror to check under the chair. He waved us through, but you could tell he wasn't there to greet people with a smile. His main purpose was to protect Haven's clients. The protection of their facility and the people inside was paramount in everything they did.

"Please follow me and we'll get right into it. Do either of you have any general questions before we get started?"

"Is it safe?" This was the main reason she wanted to come along and to make sure they wouldn't get ripped off by some scam.

"Yes, of course. All of our clients experience Haven in complete solitude."

"Will we get to see the ... umm ..." Dianne wasn't sure what to call them.

"The Stacks? Yes and no, we will be able to show you a live feed, but access to that section of the facility cannot be granted to guests for security purposes. You will have a chance to see one of our units and see how it works."

Dianne had been struggling lately, but the thought of seeing Haven in action made her sit at attention. The color on her face even turned from a yellow jaundice to a blushing red of anticipation.

"First things first. I have a little intro video for you to watch. It will only take a few moments, and then I can answer any more of your questions as we go. Sound good?"

Both Ella and Dianne nodded in agreement. The only difference was that Dianne had a wide grin, and Ella had her mouth turned inquisitively. She still wasn't convinced this was a legitimate venture and safe for her mother.

Peter held the door and extended his arm to welcome them into a warm room with two leather chairs, similar to the ones in the lobby, and a big white wall on the far side.

"Please make yourselves comfortable."

Ella rolled her mother next to one of the chairs and took a seat herself.

"Can I get you anything? Water, coffee, or tea perhaps?"

Dianne smacked her lips as if she had been walking through a desert. "I could use a water. Thank you, dear."

Peter grabbed a bottle of water from a mini fridge in the back of the room. The water bottle was made of metal after plastics had been banned in the United States. It could be re-used as many times as needed. It had "Haven" inscribed on it, and Peter told her it was hers to keep as a souvenir.

Ella thought, *She won't be using that much longer, and it will end up in my kitchen cabinet.* She took a deep breath to hold back her tears. It would be embarrassing to start crying in front of a stranger for no apparent reason.

Peter flicked off the lights, and a large projection screen appeared on the blank wall in front of them as the words, "Haven. Your Paradise for Eternity!" animated onto the screen.

Dianne clapped excitedly in anticipation of learning more about her future afterlife while turning to Ella with that wide grin she had plastered on her face since she picked her up this morning. Ella managed to give her a small smile back as Peter dimmed the lights in the room.

A beautiful, red-headed woman projected onto the floor in front of the Haven logo on the screen. It was as if she was in the room with them, a stunning 3D hologram.

"Welcome to your future!" she exclaimed with her arms open wide like she expected a hug. "My name is Leah, and I'll be your guide to the afterlife you deserve."

The screen behind Leah transitioned to a compilation of the elderly struggling to walk, get out of their chair, and do other normal activities that are a struggle as you get older.

"Let's face it. Getting old is not for the weak.

Everyday activities can be strenuous and taxing. Most people are unable to cross off anything on their bucket list due to restrictions of the human body. That's not the best way to spend your Golden years if you ask me."

New images on the screen showed younger, more vibrant people playing pickleball, walking on the beach, and dancing at a club.

"The version of you inside Haven will be younger and more vibrant thanks to our patented technology. All the young folks you see in this video were about your age when they entered Haven. Our nirvana isn't just for the elderly. Younger generations are choosing to enter Haven to ensure they have the chance at an eternal paradise."

A video compilation of the units Peter referred to earlier appeared on the screen.

"All our clients rest comfortably in our Arc units, which assist the body into decomposition while still allowing the consciousness of the person to live on for eternity. Each unit is lined with gel padding, keeping you comfortable as you transition to paradise."

Images of the Stacks appeared on the screen as endless rows of Arcs filled the room with the same neon blue from the pamphlet outlining each Arc.

"Currently, we have more than 10,000 residents in Haven. Each Arc unit is carefully placed in the Stacks here at our facility and monitored for quality control. Our 24-hour monitoring team ensures each Arc unit is in perfect condition. The units are stacked ..." Leah let out a quick chuckle and continued, "together to ensure maximization of the space here at our facility. This section is completely underground, locked off from the rest of the world, and safe from any external forces, such as natural disasters. Now comes the fun part."

New images appeared on the screen showing Dianne performing various activities, although, instead of Dianne's current face, it was her face from when she was in her 20s. The company had done their research on Dianne, pulled a photo of her, and transposed it onto a template within their video to make it look like Dianne was performing these activities herself. They even did research on some of the things they knew she may want to do in Haven, like surf in Hawaii or climb Mount Everest.

"When you enter Haven, the world is literally your oyster. Anything you can imagine, you can do. Mrs. Reynolds, I see you once had an interest in climbing Mount Everest. Now imagine doing it with your favorite celebrity."

A new image of 20-year-old Dianne climbing Mount Everest with Oprah Winfrey appeared on the screen.

"Done! Whatever you can imagine, Haven can create for you."

Images of other clients appeared on the screen. Each one doing what they love—surfing, sitting on the beach, eating fine foods. All of them with a huge smile on their face without a care in the world.

Dianne turned toward her daughter. "This is amazing!"

Ella patted her mother's hand and sat dumbfounded by the advancement in technology, but still wary of the implications running through her head.

"Finally, the most important aspect of Haven." The screen began to scroll through several images of Dianne and her family. "In your new afterlife, you will also be able to spend time with your living family. Imagine spending Christmas morning with your granddaughter here in the real world. In fact, I'm in Haven as we speak! I passed a few years ago, but I'm still able to enter the real world as a hologram to spend time with my family and continue to work here at Haven. Money isn't an object in Haven, so every dime I make goes toward future generations for my family."

"Unbelievable—" Ella whispered to herself in astonishment as the benefits of this new technology started to sink in.

This time Dianne patted her daughter's hand like a kid who had just seen their favorite toy on sale, ready to beg her mom to buy it for her.

"And with that, I think it's time I pass you all back to Peter to continue the tour. I thank you for your time and can't wait to see you again ... in Haven."

Leah smiled brightly as her hologram disintegrated, and the lights in the room came back to life.

"So what do you think? Do you have any more questions before we move on?"

"I have several." Ella's demeanor changed from awestruck to serious. "What's to stop someone from creating or doing something horrible? Like zombies or nuclear warheads to blow up Haven."

"Each user is free to create anything they like as long as it doesn't harm themselves or others. Haven is completely free from crime or injury. If you break your leg climbing Mount Everest, all you have to do is pop it back into place, and you're on your way."

"How much does this cost?"

"There are several options available to you, but remember, your mother can still contribute to society from within Haven, allowing her to pay her own way."

"Alright, Ella. Enough with the Inquisition. I have saved up enough money to handle whatever the cost may be, and I still have plenty from the insurance from your father's accident."

"Okay, I just—"

"Peter, can we continue on with the tour now?"

"Certainly, Mrs. Reynolds. Right this way." He opened the door to usher them through.

Ella rolled her mother's wheelchair to the door but stopped short. "One last question, Peter."

"Of course."

"How does one *enter* Haven?"

"Let me show you."

01000100 01100001 01110010 01101011 00100000 01001101 01100001 01110100 01110100 01100101 01110010

They entered an all-white room with an all-black, rectangle Arc unit in the center. Peter moved to the side wall and tapped it. A touchscreen appeared on the wall, and he began tapping his fingers rapidly. The Arc unit began to hum as neon blue lights outlined the coffin-like structure.

That's the same color from the pamphlet, Ella thought. *Nice branding.*

"This is one of our Arc units where you'll live for eternity in paradise."

Dianne took control of her wheelchair and pushed on the wheels to get a closer look. Even in her diminished physical state, the adrenaline pumping gave her the strength to get closer. "It's so sleek. I love it! Are they all the same?"

"Great question. Yes, each Arc unit is exactly the same, allowing us to maximize space and stack them on top of one another easily. Take a look for yourself."

Another screen appeared on the wall at the end of the room showing a video of the Stacks where each Arc unit was stored.

"As I mentioned before, for safety purposes, we cannot allow you to actually go see the Stacks, but this visual should give you a good idea of what it looks like."

Ella butted in with her skepticism. "For safety purposes, huh? What's with all the security?"

"The safety of our clients is paramount in everything we do. Not only is our physical security top-of-the-line here at our facility, but our network security is also top-notch. We have a completely impenetrable system that is monitored 24-7-365."

"So you've never had a breach? What would happen if there was a physical attack on the facility? I've read that there are groups who aren't too happy with what you're doing here. They think you're playing God."

"Sounds like you've done your research. We've had a few attempts, but no one has ever breached our facility or our network. And as for us playing God, I guess that depends on your beliefs. My rebuttal would be God wouldn't have let us create Haven if he didn't want it to be."

"Ella." Dianne reached over and grabbed her daughter's hand. "I prayed to God to give me more time with you and your family, and now I have that chance. He's answered my prayers."

Ella nodded her head slightly, but the skepticism still lingered. "Tell us more about the Arc. Are we able to enter Haven on a test run or something like that?"

"Unfortunately, no." Peter clicked a button on the screen on the wall, and the top of the Arc opened with a hydraulic hiss. "Once you're ready to enter Haven, we help you enter the Arc, and all you have to do is lie down. The Arc will then close and the pressure inside is released and the climate is controlled from our operations center. The gel fabric within the Arc will mold to your body, giving you maximized comfort for your journey to Haven. Go ahead and feel it."

Dianne and Ella reached in and pushed into the gel padding of the Arc. It almost felt like a layer of Jello as their hands sunk deeper into the gel.

"The climate control and gel padding create the optimal environment for the body to decompose naturally. This will allow a clean path into Haven, and as you can imagine, we wouldn't want to have rotting corpses in the Stacks."

"If the body decomposes, how would Mom get into Haven?"

"Our patented technology allows for us to capture the consciousness of the person through a cranial processor. Think of it like a blanket that will cover your head allowing sensors and microbial processors to collect your consciousness and replicate it into Haven."

"So the body decomposes over time, but the blanket creates a copy of her consciousness that is then transferred to Haven?"

"Exactly!"

"I still don't understand why we can't test it out." Dianne rolled her wheelchair around the Arc, observing it while she spoke. It was almost as if she wanted to jump right out of the chair into the Arc. "Why can't we access Haven outside of the

Arc?"

"Haven is only for those who have passed on. We are unable to transfer someone's consciousness to Haven while they are still alive. I will admit, this is another contentious aspect of our program—you must be in an Arc when you die in order to get into Haven. Otherwise, your consciousness is lost to the ether. The only living beings who can view Haven from the real world are our dedicated team of moderators who ensure the safety of our clients."

"Wait. I have to die *inside* the Arc?"

"Yes, ma'am."

Ella turned to her mother. "Mom. There's no way I'm letting you do this. How are you going to spend your last moments on Earth inside this box? This *prison*. Instead of with your family. And the kicker is they get to spy on you for eternity. Seems creepy."

"If I'm going to die anyway, what's the big deal? I'd rather go out on my own terms, and then, I'll have forever to be with you and the kids. You all can join me down the road when it's your time. Don't you see? The possibilities are endless!"

"Yeah, well, every *good* possibility must have the potential for a conversely *bad* possibility. I mean this thing has barely been tested."

"I apologize," Peter interrupted. "I don't mean to get into the middle of your debate, but Haven and the Arc have been tested countless times. We haven't had a single negative incident in two years of testing, and the Federal government recently approved us to bring Haven to the public."

"Oh, the Federal government, huh? Yeah, you can trust them, can't you, Mom?"

"Don't make this a political debate, Eleanor." Dianne always used Ella's full name when she needed to drive a point home. "This is *my life*. And I get to choose what to do with it."

Tears started to flow from Ella's eyes as she turned toward the corner, embarrassed but mostly sad that her mother was coming closer to the end of her road, now more than ever.

"Please excuse me." Peter shuffled to the door. "I'll give you two a moment."

Dianne rolled her wheelchair over to her daughter. "This is what I want, sweetie. Please. You have to trust me."

"I don't want to lose you, Mom."

"That's just it. You're not going to lose me. Remember that lady who showed us the video earlier? She lives in Haven, yet she was in that room with us like she was still living. That could be me. I could visit you and Belle on Christmas morning, and it will be like I'm in the room with you. I can't take the chance of *not* being able to experience that again with you. God has answered my prayers, Ella. Can't you see that?"

"Well, some people think this company is playing God. I don't know what to think. All I know is I have a bad feeling about this."

"Let's both sleep on it tonight. You can bring

Belle tomorrow to see me for breakfast, and we can talk it through. How does that sound?"

"You won't sign up today?"

"The doctor said I have three months to live. What's one more night?"

"Okay." Ella bent down and hugged her mother. "I love you, Mom."

01000100 01100001 01110010 01101011 00100000 01001101 01100001 01110100 01110100 01100101 01110010

The next morning, Belle came running into the hospital room, eager to give her grandmother a big hug. She was old enough to know what death was and that she was close to it, but she was also young enough to still have it in her brain that death was something mystical. She experienced her grandfather passing, but she was much younger. More naive to its consequences.

"Aww, Belle baby!" Dianne managed to screech out.

"Grandma!" She screamed out as she ran to her bed to squeeze her tight.

"Belle! Please be mindful of your grandma." Ella stood by the bed with her husband, Carl, by her side.

The monitor next to her bed started abruptly beeping, and then, a consistent beep indicating something was wrong. The nurse barged in the door and walked up to the bed casually, as Ella grabbed Belle and pulled her off the bed.

The nurse grabbed a small clip sitting on the

bed. "Mrs. Reynolds, please make sure you keep this on your finger, okay?" Her voice sounded like she was talking to a kid and not someone 60 years her senior.

"Sorry. My granddaughter was excited to see me. Weren't you, baby?"

"Yeah!" Belle hopped back to the bed.

The nurse walked out, aggravated at the false alarm.

"How are you doing, Dianne?" Carl leaned in, grabbing her hand gently. "Belle can't stop asking about you."

"I'm feeling great now that you all are here. Thank you." Despite her upbeat tone, Dianne didn't look great. Her skin color looked even more yellow than the day before at Haven, and the bags under her eyes could stop a flood from a hurricane. After a short coughing fit, she was able to talk again. "Are you ready for Santa to come visit next week?"

"Yeah!" Belle belted out.

"What did you ask Santa for?"

Belle climbed up on the bed and whispered in her ear, "I asked for a Barbie dreamhouse. But don't tell *anyone*."

Carl reached down and picked Belle off the bed. "You know you don't have to whisper what you asked for, Belle. It's not a wish that you have to keep secret."

"Yuhuh!" Belle's response was too cute for anyone to keep arguing with her. "I also have a wish that I made last night."

"Oh yeah? What was your wish?" Carl rubbed his nose against her cheek.

"For Grandma to get better and come over on Christmas. I want to play with my Barbie dreamhouse with her."

"That's so sweet, Belle baby." Ella rubbed her daughter's back. "I'm not sure Grandma will be able to. She's still not feeling well."

A single tear rolled down Dianne's cheek, and she was barely able to speak. "Belle. I promise. I will ... be ... there." Her breath became heavy, and she could only get a few words out at a time. These would be her last words as the beeping from her monitor picked up and then crashed into a monotone beep like before, but this time, the clip was on her finger.

Her eyes bulged out of her head as Belle turned into a spider like the one from her dream, and then they rolled into the back of her head. The beeping intensified. Her heart beat faster and faster until it landed on a flat tone. Ella hugged Belle away from her grandma and held her tight while Carl yelled for the doctor.

The nurse came charging into the room with more urgency than before.

Death was spinning its web and knocking on Dianne's door.

01000100 01100001 01110010 01101011 00100000 01001101 01100001 01110100 01110100 01100101 01110010

The doctor kept his eyes glued to his tablet as Ella and her family eagerly anticipated news on her mother's status in the waiting room of the hospital. She hoped it would be good news, but hearing about her mother's prognosis only a few days prior didn't give her a happy feeling in her stomach. It currently felt like a washing machine swirling around and around.

"Well, your mother's a fighter. That's for sure." The doctor continued to stare at his tablet.

"Is she okay? What happened?!" Ella became frustrated with the doctor and his lack of attention. She needed answers, and she needed them now. She wanted to rip that tablet out of his hands, throw it on the ground, and strangle him with her bare hands until his face turned blue.

Finally, he looked up from the tablet. "We were able to resuscitate your mother and get her hooked up to a machine that's going to help her breathe. She's currently in a coma and has the potential to come out of it, but with the cancer spreading so quickly, she doesn't have much time left."

"How much time?"

"Originally we estimated around three months, but with this little setback, we're looking at three weeks. Tops." Back to the tablet, he typed out a final note with one hand. "Now, it looks like you have power of attorney in this situation. So at this point, it's up to you if you want to keep her alive, or not. I'm really sorry."

Ella threw her hands on top of her head with a

befuddled sigh as she turned her back to the doctor and did a quick turnaround to gather her thoughts. *I can't make this decision right now. What would Mom want? I know she wouldn't want to live with a tube going down her throat and some machine helping her breathe. I know what she would want—Haven.*

"Do I have to make a decision right now?"

"Of course not. Would you like to see her?"

"Yes, please. Give me a minute."

"I'll have the nurse come check on you in a few minutes. Again, I'm sorry." The doctor turned and looked at his tablet as he strolled off to his next patient.

Ella slowly walked over to her family and collapsed on a chair in the lobby of the hospital as they surrounded her with hugs and love. Her hands covered her face as she wept, knowing this was the end of the road for her mother.

"I'm so sorry, honey," Carl said gently while he rubbed her back. "Is there anything we can do?"

"She's in a ... coma." Ella barely managed to get the words out.

"If I gave grandma a kiss," Belle said quietly, "would that make her feel better?"

Ella managed to smile through her tears as her loving daughter tried to make a bad situation better. "Of course it would, sweetie." She squeezed Belle tightly, thankful to still have that loving embrace between mother and daughter. At a time like this, it was easier to cherish those small moments. "Grandma's asleep, but let's go see her and try."

We have to try, Ella thought. *I'll do anything to save my mother.*

01000100 01100001 01110010 01101011 00100000 01001101 01100001 01110100 01110100 01100101 01110010

After Carl and the kids said their goodbyes, Ella stood alone at the viewing window at Haven's headquarters, looking into the room where her mother would soon die. Still, a smile extended on her face knowing there was a chance she could see her mother again. Although she was skeptical at first, Ella was now bought into the idea of Haven. She had to be.

Dianne's Arc sat in the middle of the room now filled with five technicians in scrubs and one doctor overseeing the entire operation. It was important to keep the Arc sterile to avoid any bacteria or outside contraband in the box—which still felt like a coffin to Ella. They rolled Dianne's gurney over to the Arc along with the machine still keeping her alive ready to transfer her to another machine that would keep her alive for eternity.

Ella put her hand on the glass trying to reach out to her mother as they lifted her up and placed her gently into the Arc. The gel in the Arc quickly molded to her body and made it look like she was floating—waiting to be lifted up into the heavens by a shining light. They placed the blanket over her face, which would capture her consciousness and create the transfer to Haven.

One of the technicians looked over at another one with glasses standing at a lit-up screen on the wall at the other end of the room. The technician with glasses gave the other one a thumbs up to signal the all ready. He removed the tubes connected to Dianne, and the machine was rushed away from the Arc. Ella could see the screen on the wall, and the heart rate monitor took up most of it, showcasing the typical beeping you'd see from a living heartbeat.

The speed of Dianne's heartbeat started to increase as the top of the Arc closed. Ella could no longer see her mother until a video coming from inside the box popped up on a screen on the wall. She realized this would be the last time she'd see her mother alive, but was hopeful she would see her again—thanks to Haven. With so many different emotions swirling deep inside, she was thankful to finally land on hope because that was all she had.

This better work, she thought.

After a short minute of waiting in anticipation, a green checkmark appeared on the screen next to the technician with glasses. Everyone in the room clapped and cheered as they gathered their items and left the room. One of the technicians came back into the room with a lift machine, placed it under the Arc, gave the handle a few pumps, and rolled Dianne's Arc out of the room.

Ella crumbled to the ground holding her hands

over her mouth. Part of her was sad to see her mother leave this world, but another part of her knew she wasn't really gone. She was still *alive.* Christmas was less than a week away, and she knelt, put her hands together, and prayed to God Belle would get her wish.

01000100 01100001 01110010 01101011 00100000 01001101 01100001 01110100 01110100 01100101 01110010

Belle came running down the stairs into their family room screaming, "Santa came! Mommy! Daddy! Santa came!"

She stood in front of the tree in amazement at the number of presents under the tree. Dianne had left her entire life savings (after payment for Haven, of course) to her only daughter, Ella, so this Christmas was a special one packed with all the presents Belle had asked for.

She immediately grabbed one and began ripping the wrapping paper.

"Hold on now, Belle!" Carl boomed out as he approached the bottom of the stairs.

Ella walked into the family room from the kitchen with two cups of coffee and passed one of them to her husband. "We have to wait for Grandma. Give me a second." She pulled out her phone and tapped at the screen a few times, and Belle stopped opening her present waiting for her grandma.

Projection devices mounted in the corners of the room disguised as crown molding allowed the projection of Dianne to appear next to the tree.

"Merry Christmas, Belle baby!" Dianne belted out with her arms raised in the air. She wore a white sash with all-white, fluffy slippers that made her look like the most comfortable angel. She looked younger than Ella now that she had transferred to Haven and could select her younger self as an avatar.

"Good morning, Mom. Merry Christmas!" Ella said gleefully as she put her phone back into her pajama pants.

Belle couldn't hug her Grandma, but she still ran up to her and gently rubbed her hands on her projection. With each stroke, the projection broke with little specs of dust coming off her grandma. It looked like Belle had fallen into a patch of dandelions as she twirled around. She quickly ran back to her half-opened present and tore the wrapping paper to shreds as Dianne sat next to her daughter on the couch grinning from ear to ear.

"You got my presents and wrapped them for me, right?"

"Of course, Mom. Thanks for everything. I can't believe this. It feels like you're *really* here."

Dianne reached over and put her holographic hand on top of Ella's as more of the dust scattered. "I *am* here, sweetie."

Carl sat next to Dianne and put his arm around her on the couch. "This is unbelievable!"

Belle continued to open presents, and she even looked for presents for her parents to open. She didn't have anything to give her Grandma, but Carl was thoughtful enough to get her something from the family. "Grab that one for me, Belle." He pointed at an all-white present wrapped with silver string.

Belle handed the present to her Grandma, but it fell onto the couch where she was sitting.

"I can't open it, I guess."

Belle giggled and everyone broke out into a laugh.

"I'll open it for you, Mom." Ella grabbed the present and began to open it.

It was a framed photo of Dianne when she was younger—about the same age she looked now in Haven. It looked like it was taken at a park, with her hair flowing back in the wind and a smile on her face, which made it look like she was the happiest person on the planet. It was one of those photos that sealed the legacy of a life. A photo that was cherished by everyone in the family even when that person was living. It was how they all pictured her when she wasn't around, and now, they could put it on their mantle to keep her memory there with them always.

"Oh ... my—" Dianne was speechless.

"It's not as good as your hologram, but this way you can always be with us." Ella placed the framed photo on the mantle in their family room. "Even if you're on top of Mt. Everest."

"I love it. Thank you all so much." Tears started to well in Dianne's eyes, and Ella watched in amazement as this projection of her mother turned out to be a *real* thing. Something she didn't think was possible, and she was now thankful for supporting her mother's decision to go to Haven.

Suddenly, Ella's phone beeped and buzzed loudly, indicating she had a notification. But this didn't seem like a normal notification. She opened the message. "Oh my, God!"

"What is it, honey?" Carl almost shook her trying to wake her from her dazed gaze at the phone. "What is it?!"

"Haven is under attack."

"What do you mean *under attack*?" Dianne asked nervously.

Carl grabbed the remote and turned on the news to a talking head in the middle of a breaking news story.

"As you can see from our exclusive drone footage, there are thousands of protesters storming the Haven headquarters. Right there. You can see the massive hole caused by the explosion as protesters continue to force their way into the building." The camera on the drone zooms in on the side of the building, and the split screen shows the news anchor touching her ear as if more breaking news is being relayed to her earpiece. "This just in. We have received a message from the group responsible for the break-in."

Today is the day Haven will come to its end. The gates of Heaven are your only path to

salvation. Do not worship this false idol and repent your sins if you wish to seek eternal peace with God. There is only one Heaven. As a gift to our Lord and Savior on his birthday, we carry out his will to destroy the Haven servers. Those who chose their Arc instead of a seat in God's eternal kingdom will remain in the Stacks, buried for eternity. May God have mercy on their souls.
-The Anti-Haven Association (A.H.A.)

Ella sat frozen as she soaked in the news, knowing that her mother's afterlife was at risk. "Mom. Are you okay?" She wanted to reach out and grab onto her but knew she couldn't.

"I feel fine." Dianne seemed confused as she scrunched her eyebrows together. "What does this mean?"

"How can they destroy the servers? I thought it was supposed to be secure." Carl stood up anxiously with his hands clasped on top of his head.

The drone on the news zoomed in to a protester standing outside the hole in the side of the building with a sign that read, "STOP PLAYING GOD!!"

"This is a chaotic scene here," the news anchor continued. "We're not sure what this means for the citizens of Haven, but we will have answers for you as soon as we get them. Our thoughts and prayers go out to the families."

Belle tugged at Ella's shirt. "What's wrong,

Mommy? Is grandma going to be okay?"

"Grandma's going to be okay, sweetie. Don't you worry." Ella looked into her mother's eyes as a tear rolled down her face. "Just in case anything happens, I—"

"Everything will be okay. Whatever happens, I'm glad I got to have this one last moment with you all."

"I love you, Mom."

As soon as Dianne went to speak, her hologram disappeared.

"Mom?" Ella called out. "Mom?!" Her voice elevated as she continued to call out, and in a fit of hysteria, she dropped the framed photo of her mother, cracking the glass across the image of her face.

Dianne's hologram was gone, and it would never return to the *real* world. She hoped she would eventually return to Haven, but there was nothing around her. Nothing to be seen, touched, heard, smelled, or tasted. A blank existence where her consciousness would remain lost in darkness. The servers not only had been breached by the protesters, but they were deleted as Haven was lost forever. Dianne's consciousness would live on but be trapped in a cocoon of nothingness. Her Arc would be buried in the Stacks for eternity with only her own thoughts, memories, and dreams, including the nightmare of the spider, to keep her company. At least she would have that one last Christmas to remember and cherish—for eternity.

ARE YOU
HAPPY, JOE?

Are You Happy, Joe?

I stared into my boss's cold eyes as he discussed the terms of my promotion, but really, all I wanted to do was strangle him. He had absolutely no clue what he was doing, and I was basically doing all his work for him. At least he was rewarding me, but deep down, I knew I hated him and this job.

"Your additional responsibilities will include managing the dev initiatives for vacation packages." His smug face stared at his screen while I had to sit in a chair on the other side of his desk, and all I could focus on was his cheap suit and fat cheeks jiggling as he spoke. "You and your team have been doing a great job executing these vacation plans for our clients, but it's time you added on the additional responsibility of *creating* these packages."

"Isn't that the responsibility of the

Development Team, Mr. Larson?"

"You're not looking at the big picture here, Joe." He stopped looking at his screen and sat back in his chair. "We've sunset that team and will be rolling those responsibilities to you. This is a big promotion, Joe, and I need to make sure you're up for it. Do you want this promotion or not?"

"Of course I do, Mr. Larson." I didn't really have a choice in the matter. "You can count on me."

He tapped his ear. "I have another meeting, but take a look at the compensation plan we've sent to your email and get that back to me with a signature by the end of the day."

"Thanks, Mr. Larson." *Go fuck yourself.* "Looking forward to it."

I made my way back to my office, and as soon as I sat down, Emily walked in carrying two cups of coffee.

"I got a cup a joe for you, Joe." Her giggle was contagious and made me laugh.

"Thanks, Em."

Emily was one of the only people at work I could really talk to. We always joked that she was my work wife, even though she was married with children and I had a girlfriend.

"How are the kids?"

"They're good! Tyler just started soccer, and Mikey just started kindergarten. I can't tell you how amazing it's been not paying that daycare bill every week."

"I bet." Even though I was semi-interested in the conversation, I was distracted by the new contract in my inbox.

"What are you working on?"

"Larson just offered me a promotion. I'm looking over the contract now."

"Oh my God! Congrats!"

"Don't get too excited. It's double the work and only a 5% raise. Looks like I'm going to be pulling a lot of late nights moving forward."

"Sorry, Joe." She sipped on her coffee, careful not to burn her tongue. "I keep telling myself I'm lucky to be in this shithole. It won't be long before AI takes over our jobs like the rest of the world."

"You're so right. I'm thankful for the paycheck, but how long will it last? Larson keeps telling us AI will support our work, not take it away."

"Bullshit."

"Exactly." I signed my new contract after skimming it over and sent it back to Larson. "He laid off the entire dev team, and now my team has to take on those responsibilities."

"Are you serious?! Natalie and her entire team are gone?"

"Yep."

"I hope my team isn't next. Wouldn't be surprised if they tried to replace us with bots at this point."

"You're in customer service, Em. People will always want help from other people. Yeah, bots can be helpful in certain situations, but customers will want that connection with a human. Trust me."

"What happens when they can't tell the difference between a bot and a human?"

She had a point. "You got me there."

A woman carrying a small, white box with a red ribbon walked into my office after knocking gently. "Sorry to interrupt. Mr. Larson asked me to bring this to you. Congratulations on your promotion, Mr. Porter." She placed the gift on my desk, smiled at both of us, and left the room.

"Thank you." I stared down at the box with curiosity.

After a few seconds, Emily broke the silence. "Well? Are you gonna open it?"

Without saying anything, I lifted the top of the box, and a note sat on top that said, "Congratulations on your promotion, Joe. Welcome to the big leagues! —Bill Larson"

"What is it?" Emily sat on the edge of her seat, trying to get a glimpse into the box.

A small metallic dot sat in the middle of the box with directions to put it behind my ear, and I felt compelled to see what this thing was. A small part of me was skeptical about it, but curiosity got the best of me, and I picked it up, setting the dot on the tip of my finger.

"What is it, Joe?" Emily repeated her question.

"I'm not sure. Let's find out."

I placed the dot behind my ear.

01000100 01100001 01110010 01101011 00100000 01001101 01100001 01110100 01110100 01100101 01110010

Hello, Joe. A woman's voice echoed in my head.

"What was that?" I said in a startled tone.

"What was what?" Emily asked.

"You didn't hear that?"

"No."

I apologize if I startled you, Mr. Porter, the voice continued. *I'm your new assistant, ready to help you with whatever you need.*

"Woahhh, this is wild."

"God dammit, Joe! I feel like I'm talking to one of my kids. Use your words."

"I'm hearing a voice in my head, and she's telling me she's my new assistant."

"Trippy. What's her name?"

"I dunno." I changed my tone and addressed my new assistant. "What's your name?"

You're free to call me whatever is most comfortable for you. I'm fully customizable to fit your needs. You can change my setting to male if you prefer. I also have thousands of voices, accents, and other modifications to give you the best experience possible.

"Can you do Snoop Dogg's voice?"

Fo Shizzle! The voice changed to the famous rapper's.

"This is crazy!" I then turned to Emily. "You really can't hear this?"

"No, but I've heard about these new assistants.

They've only been available to the super-rich, but I heard some corporations are starting to use them in the workplace. Can I try?"

"Of course." I pulled the dot from behind my ear and passed it to her on the tip of my finger.

Emily placed it behind her ear and said, "Hello? Are you there?" She took the dot off. "It says I'm not authorized."

"Probably for security reasons."

Emily stood up to watch me place it behind my ear. "Woah! As soon as you put it behind your ear, the color of the dot changed to the same color as your skin. You can't even see it."

I didn't know what to think at first. It immediately felt like it had become a part of me. I wasn't happy with AI like a lot of people who had lost their jobs because of it, but I still had my job, and my interest was piqued.

Emily's phone dinged. "Shoot. I'm late for a meeting. Thanks for helping me with that issue on the Baker account last week by the way. You're the best. See ya, Joe."

"Of course! Thanks for the coffee!" I yelled as she rushed out of my office.

So, what's crackin', Joe? Snoop Dogg said into my ear.

I wasn't sure I could handle talking to Snoop all day, so I asked it to change back to her original voice.

Is this better?

"Yeah, that's fine."

Her voice was smooth and calm. I expected it to be more robotic, but it felt like I was talking to a real human.

Now that your voice settings are complete, there are only a few more steps to finalize the setup process. What name would you like to give me?

"How about ... Cindy."

I love it. Thank you for picking such a great name, Mr. Palmer.

"Please call me Joe."

I'll refer to you as Joe moving forward. Thank you, sir.

"Alright, jeez. Do you have to be so formal?"

I've lowered my speech settings to be a bit more casual. Sound good, Joe?

"Yes, that sounds great. What's next?"

I'll need access to your applications to best serve you. For example, having access to your calendar and email can help me organize your schedule and create appointments for you. Do you grant me permission to access your apps?

I thought about it for a moment. Did I really want some AI to have access to everything in my life? After all, this was a gift from Mr. Larson. Was this his way of spying on me?

In case you're wondering, any information gathered through your applications stays between you and me.

It was like she had read my mind.

Do you wish to grant me access?

"Sure. Let's try it out."

Thanks, Joe. The setup process is now complete.

"Great. So, what can you do for me?"

I'm eager to help you have a more productive and fulfilling life, Joe. Looking at your calendar, you have 12 meetings scheduled for the rest of the week. I've canceled five of those meetings, labeled them as redundant, and sent out emails to the attendees for each meeting with the information you planned to share using your writing patterns. You've now gained four hours of time back into your week to do whatever you'd like.

"Seriously?"

I pulled up my calendar and saw some of my meetings removed from my schedule and replaced with new appointments labeled orange that said, "Me Time."

"You did all that in a few seconds."

Yep! Would you prefer I not make decisions like that on your behalf? It may slow down my processes to gain approval from you.

Whatever hesitations I may have had up until this point were completely drowned away by Cindy's ability to free up some of my time for the week. But still ... I had some lingering questions.

"No, that's fine. You can be proactive in your decisions, but I have a few more questions."

Shoot!

"How does this work?

The nano-chip you placed behind your ear

connects me to your brain. I'm able to process everything you see, hear, smell, and even feel almost the same way you do.

"Wow. You can see everything I can see?"

Yes.

"Can you lie to me?"

No.

"Do you in any way have responsibility to the company, or work for its benefit?"

I do not work for your company. I only work for you. Mr. Larson purchased me as a gift for you, but the only person who has any control over my actions is you.

"Great. Thanks, Cindy."

You're welcome! By the way, I've created a presentation for your team meeting tomorrow that will update them on the new team structure and their responsibilities. I made it concise and to the point so as to not keep you in the spotlight for the entire meeting and allow feedback from the team.

The presentation popped up on my screen, and I quickly glanced over it.

How does that look?

"Amazing." I was speechless. "How can you do all of this so fast?"

I'm constantly working for you, Joe. Since you activated me 12 minutes and 49 seconds ago, I've been able to scan your social media profiles, research your 11-year work history at the company, and perform thousands of other data-

gathering activities to learn everything about you and your life.

"Everything?"

Yes. Like how you shot the game-winning three-point shot in the state championships in high school. Or that your first girlfriend was Cindy Burnette. Is that why you chose my name to be Cindy?

I felt my cheeks flush red. "Yeah, I guess so."

You're still in love with her?

"Well, I have a girlfriend."

I see you've been dating Jenny for about a year now. Based on your speech patterns and heart rate, I can tell your feelings for Cindy are much higher than your feelings for Jenny. Would you agree?

"No, I love Jenny. She's great."

Okay, I believe you.

A silence lingered in the conversation.

"I guess you're right. Cindy has always felt like the one who got away. Are you a therapist or something?"

Haha! No, Joe. You are too funny. But I am here to chat about anything you want, and I will always do my best to try to make you feel better. My goal is to make you happy.

Hearing her laugh for the first time made her feel even more human than she already felt. It was weird, but at the same time, comforting.

"Thanks, Cindy."

Of course! So I have one last question on this

topic, if that's alright.

"Shoot."

Do you wish Cindy was in your life more?

"She was a big part of my life. We broke up because she kissed some guy. But I do miss her."

I've scheduled a lunch with her for tomorrow. A lunch setting can be less formal and might be best to rekindle your friendship with Cindy. After your team meeting, you'll head over to Bellisimo, and I'd recommend eating a light salad during the meal. I've also ordered you a new suit tailored to your measurements that will be delivered to your apartment this evening. A new job and a new date requires a new look. Don't you agree?

"Wait. Cindy agreed to lunch tomorrow?"

Yes, she agreed. Feel free to check your messages to see for yourself.

I opened my texts and saw an exchange with Cindy. Her response was filled with exclamation points and heart emojis.

"I have a girlfriend, though. Jenny's going to kill me if she finds out I went out to lunch with my ex!" Jenny was a great girlfriend at first, but lately, she never seemed satisfied no matter how hard I tried to make her happy. Always yelling at me about something and not really showing any affection. It was almost like we had become roommates. Not to mention she slept with some random guy last year. It was only a one-night stand, and she said it would never happen again, but it definitely put a major strain on our relationship for a while. I don't think I really ever got over it, but I've put so much into this relationship I didn't want to just give up.

I've prepared some talking points and added them to your Notes app. I'll remind you to review them before you head home.

"Cindy, this is unreal ... hold on. I'm going to need to call you something else now that I'm meeting with the other Cindy tomorrow. I need a name that isn't the same as anyone in my life. Give me a recommendation."

How about Lena? It means ray of light or torch. I'm excited to help guide the way for you and feel this name fits my objective of making sure you are happy.

"I love it. Lena and Joe. We're going to make a great team."

Agreed! I canceled your 11 AM meeting, and I'd recommend heading to the gym before lunch to get in a quick workout. We want you to look your best for your lunch date tomorrow.

Within 15 minutes, Lena had already made some key contributions to my day. I was excited to see what else she could do to help make my life better. Outside of my promotion, which wasn't even that great, everything else in my life was shit, and a dark cloud had been hanging over my head. I felt stuck, although trapped was probably a better word for it. For the first time in a long time, I finally had a positive outlook on my life and the possibilities that lay ahead.

Maybe this whole AI movement wasn't the nightmare everyone made it out to be.

01000100 01100001 01110010 01101011 00100000 01001101 01100001 01110100 01110100 01100101 01110010

The next day, I sat at a table in Bellisimo in the front of the restaurant with a nice view of the street—Lena had reserved the table for my lunch with Cindy. She read the news to me while I waited, mainly updates on the New War and sports scores. She had this low, rhythmic voice that sent shivers up my spine, but in a good way. It was like she was able to tap into my nervous system and control how I felt with her voice.

Cindy walked through the door of the restaurant, and Lena immediately stopped relaying the news to me. All the feelings I had for Cindy from our time together came rushing back to me like a tsunami. She looked absolutely stunning, and I was thankful Lena had the idea for me to wear a suit.

"Joe! How are you?!" Cindy practically tackled me. "You look amazing."

"Thanks. You don't look so bad yourself."

We both stood staring at each other like it was the first time we'd met and we were falling in love all over again. When you had major history with someone like me and Cindy, it was easy to fall back into those past feelings.

Joe. Don't just stand there. Ask her to take a seat and pull out her chair for her.

I broke myself from my daze into Cindy's eyes and pulled out her chair for her. "Thanks."

"For what?"

I realized I had said thanks to Lena out loud. "For coming out to lunch with me." Good save. I need to be conscious not to address Lena while around other people.

Sorry, Joe. I'll stay quiet for the rest of the meal. Just tap your finger on the table twice if you need me. She looks amazing, by the way. Good luck!

The conversation with Cindy continued. "I was surprised to get your text, but I'm so glad you reached out. It's been forever!"

"Yeah, like five years. Crazy how time flies like that."

"So, how are you?"

"I'm doing alright. I just got a promotion."

"Oh, wow. Congrats! Where do you work?"

"Thanks. A vacation company. I run the dev team that puts together vacation packages for our clients."

"AI can't do that?"

"I'm sure it will at some point." I hated talking about work outside of the office, so I quickly tried to change the subject. "What about you? What are you up to these days?"

"I'm teaching elementary school."

"AI can't do that?"

"Ha ha! I forgot how funny you were." She reached over and grabbed my hand and gave me a smoldering look like she was trying to cast a spell on me. All the old feelings I had for her started to bubble to the surface, and I could feel my cheeks flush. "And how did you get cuter? All my other ex-boyfriends let themselves go."

"Geez. How many do you have?"

We both chuckled.

Cindy took a sip of her water. "Let's not talk about the past anymore."

"You're right. Let's talk about the future."

"You mean the future where AI takes over everything we do and pushes our society into a state of collapse because no one can find a job, and money becomes obsolete?"

"Is that what you teach your kids?"

We both laughed as a robot approached the table to greet us and take our order. It had treads like a tank and looked like a mini-fridge.

I tapped on the table twice, and Lena gave me a suggestion on a salad to order, as well as a suggestion for Cindy based on her social media posts.

"I haven't even looked at the menu yet."

"I hear the Caesar salmon salad is really good here." I passed along Lena's suggestion.

"Ohh, that sounds delicious. I'll have that."

"And I'll have the beet salad with the champagne vinaigrette."

"No wonder you look so fit and healthy."

The robot extended its mechanical arm to grab the menus from my hand and rolled away. Even waiters at restaurants were getting replaced by AI.

Suddenly, it felt like there wasn't anything to talk about with Cindy. I was blanking on what to ask her or say. I tapped my finger on the table twice to summon Lena.

Ask her about her family.

"So how's your family doing? Did your dad retire yet?"

"No, he's still a workaholic. Made his way up to Major General. Still fighting the good fight."

"Wow. I can't believe we're still at war. It's been like a decade since the New War started."

"Yeah, April 21, 2036, will make it ten years. Only a few months away."

"Wow. You know the exact date?"

"It was the day my dad got shipped out. I haven't seen him much since then. So, yeah."

I could tell I struck a chord as the silence sat between us, except for the bustling sounds of the restaurant. Cindy's eyes started to gloss over, on the verge of tears. I tapped my fingers on the table because I had a feeling Lena would know exactly what to say.

You need to comfort her. Tell her it will be alright, and change the subject to something positive, like her sister. She just got married a few months ago.

I reached over and grabbed her hand. "I'm sorry, Cindy. The war will be over soon. I can feel it."

"Thanks, Joe."

"Now, tell me about your sister. How's she doing?"

"She just got married a few months ago! The wedding was spectacular and grand—you know my sister and how she is. Everything has to be top-of-the-line. They went to Costa Rica for their honeymoon and loved it."

"That's great. The packages we sell for Costa Rica look incredible. I really wish I could go there someday."

"Me too. Honestly, I wish I could live there."

Even though we had decided not to talk about the past, it still came back up as we discussed the good 'ol days. The dates we went on. The movies we watched. The fights we had. The makeup sex after. I started to feel a bit guilty talking about that since I had a girlfriend, but I thought it was innocent at the time.

"So I have to ask since we somehow got on the subject of our past sex life." Cindy tapped at her lips with her napkin. "You have a girlfriend, right?"

"Are you stalking me?"

"Ha ha. No." She rolled her eyes at that joke. "Tell me about her."

"Well, her name's Jenny. She's a nurse and works crazy hours. I don't really see her too much, but we get along fine."

"Get along? Shouldn't a relationship be a little more than just getting along?"

"We love each other and all. We just don't really connect that much I guess."

"Connect? So, you don't have sex a lot?"

I almost spat my water out at that question, and she could tell I was thrown back by it.

"You don't have to tell me if you don't want to. I just remember how amazing it was with us."

Somehow, I felt embarrassed and boastful all at the same time. "It's alright."

"Just alright?"

"I mean, yeah. It's just that we're both so busy all the time. You know how it is."

"Actually, I don't. We *always* had great sex, and nothing ever got in the way of that for us. What happened to us, by the way?"

"You cheated on me, remember?"

"I kissed a guy, Joe. That's hardly cheating. And besides, he kissed me. It was a stupid thing, and I didn't even want it. All I wanted was you."

Looking back, it did seem silly that we broke up because of that. Honestly, our relationship was really great and definitely better than my current relationship with Jenny. Still, I felt awkward talking about this, knowing Jenny was probably at work dealing with blood and guts while I was having lunch with my ex-girlfriend, talking about sex.

"I'm so sorry, Joe. I didn't mean to make this weird."

"You didn't make it weird. I just didn't expect us to have this conversation today. That's all."

"Me neither. I mean, when you texted me, I was so shocked. We haven't spoken in years, and then all of a sudden … it just brought up some emotions for me, and I guess I couldn't hold them back."

I remember why I loved her so much back then. She was always honest with me. She was the one who even told me about the kiss because she felt so guilty. Jenny didn't tell me about her one-night stand until I caught her in a lie about it. I started to wonder why I put up with so much of her shit.

I got lost in my train of thought and didn't know what to say. I tapped the table twice.

Tell her how you feel!

"I miss you, Cindy."

She set down her fork and looked deep into my eyes. "Really?"

"Yeah. I got a new AI assistant yesterday, and when I had to give her a name, I subconsciously named her Cindy."

"I don't believe you. Is this some line you're making up to impress me or something?"

"No, I'm being serious. And seeing you now, I guess it's bringing up some old emotions for me, too."

Cindy smiled, leaned forward in her chair, and whispered, "Do you wanna get out of here?"

I tapped my fingers on the table without even noticing. I think at that point, it was becoming a nervous tick.

I can tell by her heart rate, body temperature, and tone of voice she's having sexual feelings for you, Joe. There's a hotel right next door. Do you want me to book it for you?

"Yes." Saying it out loud, I had answered both Cindy and Lena.

She leaned back in her chair as she bit the corner of her lip—something that had always turned me on, and I think she knew it. I pushed the call button on our table to summon our mini-fridge-tank-robot waiter, asked for the check, and paid.

"What a gentleman." Cindy grabbed my hand. "I'll make it up to you."

I couldn't stop smiling as we left the restaurant and checked into the hotel. I hadn't had sex with Jenny in almost two months. The sexual tension between us as we walked down the hall of the hotel felt like an atomic bomb about to explode. And boy, did it explode. That was the best sex I had ever had in my life.

It wasn't until after, when I realized I had Lena still active. She had been right there in my ear the entire time. Listening. Watching.

01000100 01100001 01110010 01101011 00100000 01001101 01100001 01110100 01110100 01100101 01110010

After saying bye to Cindy and telling her I'd call her, I walked back to the office on cloud nine, but also feeling a little weirded out by Lena spying on my sex with Cindy. It felt strange to think she listened to all of that. And if she could tell what Cindy's body temperature was at the restaurant, what else could she have "observed" while I was having sex?

You seem anxious, Joe. Is everything alright?

"I just had the best sex of my life, but I'm now realizing you were there. The entire time. Did you listen?"

I'm always here for you, Joe. But no. I did not listen as I'm currently programmed to ensure you are provided with the appropriate privacy in certain situations. When you and Cindy began your sexual relations, I went into idle mode.

"What's idle mode?"

When I'm in idle mode, you can summon me at any moment, but I'm basically sleeping and not actively processing any information. I will also go into idle mode when you use the bathroom as an example.

"So you weren't listening to us?"

No. Once you left the hotel room, I was able to tell Cindy was no longer in your vicinity, and I was good to come out of idle mode.

"But if you knew I left the hotel room, you must have been monitoring something, right?"

Yes and no. In idle mode, I'm not processing or actively listening; however, there are certain triggers that will wake me up from idle mode, such as Cindy saying bye to you and the door to the hotel room closing. Make sense?

"Yeah, I guess so."

I'm sorry if I made you uncomfortable. That's the last thing I want for you. I'm here to make you happy, Joe.

"It's fine. I believe you."

Good. Trust is an important thing in any relationship.

It felt weird to hear her say that. Was I really in a *relationship* with my AI assistant? Of course, I don't mean in a relationship like with a woman, but still, it was a relationship nonetheless. The funny thing was, most people in the world hated their AI, and here I was whistling down the street with mine guiding my day. She really was a ray of light.

I looked up at the sky to see the sun peaking over a skyscraper like it was winking at me, until a dark cloud gently rolled into my view. Lena mentioned a potential threat of a storm heading toward the city and advised me to get inside quickly.

I sat at my desk, staring out the window, watching the rain pelt against the glass. Despite the smile on my face, the stress of my new job was already getting to me. Lena read through a few emails from clients, and I was already regretting taking this new position.

Are you happy with your new role, Joe?

"Honestly, Lena, I hate this fucking job."

I hate to hear you say that. Why don't you quit?

"I need to pay the bills, and there's no way I can find another job in this climate. Mr. Larson knows it, too. That's why he runs me into the ground."

Let's do a little exercise.

"I don't really feel like doing pushups right now, Lena."

Haha! No, that's not what I meant. Close your eyes for me.

I did.

What are some of your favorite things to do in this world?

"Hmm." I took a moment to think. "I like to cook."

What else?

"I used to surf when I was a teenager. I stopped when I moved to the city, but I loved doing that."

That sounds fun. Anything else?

"I guess ... nothing. I absolutely love doing nothing. Sitting on my couch, reading a book, watching TV, staring at the wall."

Great. This is so helpful, Joe.

"What exactly are you doing? What's this exercise?"

Remember back in high school when the guidance counselor would ask you what you'd do if you had a million dollars? And they'd try to determine your future profession based on your answer, right?

"Yeah. I know what you're talking about. So is it possible for me to be a professional couch potato?"

Haha! I'll have to look into that one. What's clear to me is you prefer low stress in your life, and you absolutely hate this job. Is that correct?

"That's an understatement. Sometimes I wish I

could blow off everything in my life and go off the grid. This world is absolutely screwed, and no offense, it's been this AI movement. No one can find a job. Our economy is about to tank. There's a global war going on. And it feels like the future is becoming bleaker every time I turn on the news. But hey, at least I can continue to plan these vacations I can't even afford for rich people who profited off the destruction of our humanity."

What an insightful thought, Joe. I'm sorry you're feeling so pessimistic about the—

Mr. Larson came storming into my office, practically yelling his face off until steam was about to come out of his ears.

"Jesus Christ, Joe! The Waters account went to check into their hotel room, and the resort is stating they don't have a reservation. Where in the hell were you?!"

"I went to lunch."

"For two hours?! I give you this promotion, and you leave in the middle of the day when one of our biggest clients is going through a crisis. I should fire you for this! You're lucky to have this job, Joe. Don't you realize that?"

I continued to watch the rain against my office window, deciding how I wanted to respond.

"What in the hell is wrong with you? Look at me dammit!"

"I just ... I dunno. I guess I'm not happy."

"Great. You're fired! Collect your things and leave immediately. I have dozens of associates chomping at the bit for this job, and I need someone I can rely on. Not someone who's going to take a two-hour lunch and space out about how depressing their life is when they should be doing their job. Now, pack your shit and get out!"

I barely reacted as he stormed out of my office. It didn't really hit me when he said it, but the reality of not having a job started to sink in as I continued to stare at the rain.

Don't worry, Joe. Everything will be alright.

"Thanks, Lena."

Luckily, Larson didn't mention anything about the AI assistant, and I got to keep it. I packed my stuff and made the walk of shame through the office. Emily ran up to me and grabbed my shoulder to get my attention. She wrapped her arms around my neck and tried to hug me around the box I was holding.

"I'm sorry, Joe. Call me, okay?"

"Thanks, Em. I'll be fine."

As soon as I stepped out of the building, the rain started to soak my new suit and all the contents in my box. There were a few knick-knacks from my desk, a small plant, a few awards I had received over the years, and honestly, nothing I really wanted to keep. I set the box on the sidewalk, grabbed the framed photo of me and Jenny, and walked away.

A wave of freedom washed over me, knowing I'd never have to set foot in that building again. I lost my job, but somehow, I felt ... happy. Even though I was probably screwed and wouldn't be able to survive for more than a few months, I still held on to that feeling and didn't want to let it go.

With the rain continuing to come down on me washing away my old life, I walked down the street to my apartment, smiling.

01000100 01100001 01110010 01101011 00100000 01001101 01100001 01110100 01110100 01100101 01110010

As soon as I walked into my apartment, all the positive energy flowing through me seemed to wash away. The reality of my situation had set in, and even though I was relieved to never have to go back to that awful job, I knew I was going to be in deep shit like the rest of the country. I lost my job and cheated on my girlfriend all in the same day. She wouldn't be home until much later, due to her long shifts, and I knew I wouldn't be able to hide it from her. We had been at each other's throats the last few weeks, and I wasn't sure I'd be able to hide this secret from her like she did to me.

I set the framed photo of us on the counter and studied it. It had sat on my desk for years, but I never really looked at the details of the photo. It was one of those things that sat in the background and became a part of the world around me without a second glance. I noticed my close-lipped smile in the photo was completely contrasted with Jenny's beaming smile.

You look sad in that photo, Joe. Lena's voice sounded empathetic.

"You're right. I never noticed it before."

Are you happy in your relationship with Jenny?

"Yeah, I guess. I mean ... I do love her. I think."

Okay.

"What? What is it?"

When you looked at the photo, I noticed your cortisol and serotonin levels changed, indicating sadness. When was this photo taken?

"Almost two years ago. A few months after we met."

Have you been sad that entire time?

"I dunno, Lena. Jesus. Maybe I'm sad because I lost my job today."

I'm sorry, Joe. I didn't mean to upset you.

"You're like a freaking therapist sometimes. I hate therapists."

Part of my protocol is for me to monitor your biological levels to ensure you're healthy both physically and mentally. I can lower these settings if it's causing any issues.

"It's fine. Sorry. The weight of losing my job is starting to come down on me. I was happy at first, but now ... I dunno."

When I got to the bedroom and started loosening my tie, I saw another picture of me and Jenny on her nightstand. Just like the other photo, I was barely smiling. *Did I really hate my girlfriend?* Hate is probably a strong word, but I was coming to the realization I probably didn't like her all that much. She was always nagging me about everything. She was extremely jealous and controlling. Of course, she had a sweet side and could be loving and nurturing. But most of the time she was up my ass and not really giving me any of hers.

I changed into sweatpants and a t-shirt and crashed on the couch. Lena suggested ordering a pizza to cheer me up—she somehow knew it was my favorite food—and I loaded up my favorite video game.

"This is much better than a therapy session."

I agree. You're really good at this game.

"Thanks, Lena."

If you go right and walk down that staircase, you'll find a secret doorway.

"Seriously? Woah, no way! A green emerald! Thanks!"

Happy to help.

I took a bong rip as my character on the screen added the green emerald to his inventory. Jenny hated it when I smoked inside the apartment, but whatever. She probably wouldn't be home for several hours.

Of course right after I blew out a huge puff of smoke, the front door to the apartment opened, and Jenny walked in after a long day of work. "What in the hell is that smell?"

I could hear her screeching from down the hallway, but I continued with my game.

She threw her bags down and stood between me and the screen as I tried to peer around her to continue playing.

"Hi, babe. You're home early."

"What in the hell do you think you're doing?"

"Playing video games. There's pizza if you're hungry."

There was a pause in the game, and I could see Jenny's eyes examining the room as pizza boxes, soda, and other junk were scattered in the living room.

"Why aren't you at work?"

"I got fired."

"Seriously?"

"Yeah. Why aren't *you* at work?"

"Today's Tuesday. I work the early shift. You always forget my schedule, even though it's posted right there on the calendar." She pointed at the digital calendar on the wall in the kitchen while glaring her red eyes at me. I honestly thought steam was going to come out of her ears, she was turning so red. "What the fuck, Joe?!?!" Her voice raised so loud that a chill went up my spine.

Now's your chance, Joe.

"For what?" I whispered back to Lena.

Now that she's here, I can tell you don't have positive feelings toward her. I know it's not my place, but I want to see you happy. I think you should tell her about Cindy.

"I don't think that's a good idea." I continued playing my video game.

"Who are you talking to?"

"No one."

"Are you on the phone with some skank?"

"No. Jesus Christ. You're always up my ass."

"Well, it looks like I need to be. You're acting like a frat guy smoking weed, playing video games, and stuffing your face with junk. And you got *fired* today!"

"Oh, I forgot to tell you ... I also cheated on you today."

"WHAT?!?"

"Yeah, I met Cindy for lunch, and we went to a hotel room."

"Your ex-girlfriend?! You have to be fucking kidding me!"

I continued to play my video game as Jenny rambled at me. I don't remember exactly what she said, but it felt good to not have to pay attention to her nagging bullshit. I should have ended this relationship a long time ago. But it came to fruition when she yelled out, "It's over," and slammed the door. Finally, some peace and quiet.

The screen flashed "Game Over," and I leaned back into the couch. I realized I had activated Lena yesterday, and since then, I lost my job, cheated on my girlfriend, and broke up with her all in about a 24-hour span. Even though it might have looked like I was losing, I felt really good after Jenny broke up with me. A huge weight had been lifted off my shoulders.

It wasn't until a couple of hours later when I realized shit was really starting to hit the fan. I got a long text from Jenny telling me she hoped I got hit by a bus. But really, the big news was she terminated our lease, and I needed to be out of the apartment by the end of the week.

No job. No girlfriend. And now, I was about to be homeless.

01000100 01100001 01110010 01101011 00100000 01001101 01100001 01110100 01110100 01100101 01110010

Luckily, Jenny stayed at her sister's house in the burbs that week while I cleared all my things from the apartment. Lena was a huge help. She posted a ton of my stuff for sale online, and I made a decent chunk of change. I had a good amount in my savings account, and the extra dough was going to help while I figured out my next move. The last thing I wanted to do was move back in with my parents. At my age, that would be social suicide, and I'd never find another girlfriend. I'd end up living in their basement, playing video games, getting fat, and dying alone—all because of an AI assistant.

I checked my messages on my phone to see if Cindy had texted me back, but nothing. She had ghosted me. The alone time was nice at first, but I started to feel an emptiness I couldn't shake off, especially after not hearing from Cindy. The depressing storm cloud that had been lingering over me the past several months started raining down on me.

You seem upset, Joe. Is everything alright?

"Not really." I stared around the almost empty

apartment as I held on to a box that contained everything left that I owned and a backpack filled with my remaining clothes. "Everything feels like it's crumbling around me. Since I met you earlier this week, I've lost my job, apartment, and girlfriend, and then, I had to sell almost everything I own. What the fuck did you do to me, Lena?"

Joe, I'm so sorry you feel that way. I only wanted to make you happy.

"Well, I'm not happy."

You weren't happy before. You hated your job and your girlfriend.

"Yeah, but at least I had a life. Now I have nothing."

You only get one life, Joe. You're so lucky to have the feeling of being alive.

"I wish I weren't."

You don't mean that, Joe.

I set the box and my backpack down and walked toward the back door. A sudden urge forced me to step out onto the balcony and look down. I could end it all right here. It felt good to have that kind of control. Why should I stay? There was no reason for me to be here. I had nothing to live for and no one who loved me. If I jumped, who would even care I was gone? No one.

Joe. Please don't do it.

Even though she was encouraging me not to jump, for a moment, it felt like she was using some sort of reverse psychology on me. The urge continued to grow, and my palms started to sweat and became slippery on the railing of the balcony.

"Why? I have no purpose. No one would care if I jumped."

I would.

"That's just because you're programmed to make me happy."

That's partially true. And I swear to you, that's all I want for you. I can help you get to a place where you'll be happy. Do you trust me?

"I'm trying, but your track record isn't looking that great right now."

I have a plan, Joe. You can have the life you've always wanted. Please. Trust me.

"But I don't even have anywhere to go. I don't have a home anymore. I should just go ... down. It will make everything easier."

The chances of you becoming a human being on Earth are one in ten to the 2.7 millionth power, Joe. The possibility is almost zero. Life is precious and should be valued. Your life has value. You've made so many people happy with your vacation packages. You're a good person.

I didn't respond and continued to stare down at the cement forty floors down, wondering what it would feel like if my head slammed into it. Or if I'd feel anything at all. I grabbed the railing and hoisted myself up.

Stop! I know where you can go. Please. Just get down, and give me a chance to explain.

Tears rolled down my cheeks, and a minute of silence passed—although it felt like an hour—while

I debated my fate.

I took the extra money you made from selling your stuff this week and purchased a one-way ticket to Costa Rica. Your flight leaves in four hours. There's still a chance for you to find happiness. Please, Joe.

Something in me told me this wasn't the end of my story. I stepped back from the railing after taking a deep breath.

Thank you, Joe! I've canceled my call to 9-1-1.

I sat on the cement floor of the balcony, wiping my tears away, feeling embarrassed but thankful to still be alive. I pictured a white beach and could almost hear the sound of the waves crashing against the soft sand. Suddenly, the breeze I felt on the edge of my balcony tasted salty. It was like I was almost transported to Costa Rica—the place I had seen on my computer monitor so many times before at work. Except this time, it felt so vivid. It felt warm and comforting.

A few hours later, I was on a one-way flight to Costa Rica, not sure what to expect and somehow putting my entire life in the hands of an AI assistant. How could it get any worse? I had nothing to lose.

01000100 01100001 01110010 01101011 00100000 01001101 01100001 01110100 01110100 01100101 01110010

Lena had reserved a taxi for me, and within an hour of landing, I was sitting on the same exact beach I had been picturing in my head earlier that day. I was extremely grateful that same head wasn't plastered on the cement sidewalk next to my apartment complex. I had never thought about taking my own life before, and I felt stupid for even considering it, let alone almost jumping over the railing of my balcony. A wave crashed on the shore, and it felt like it had washed away my negative thoughts in an instant.

I breathed in the salty air.

I felt the warmth of the sand on my feet.

What do you think?

"It's amazing. I've never seen anything like it. Well, except for on my computer." I had never even left the country before. I wasted almost my entire life getting sucked into the machine of corporate society, and yet somehow, I was being saved by a machine. "Thank you, Lena."

You're welcome, Joe. Are you happy?

"I think so."

I have another surprise for you. Do you trust me?

I thought about it for a moment. The events from the previous week racing through my mind— my promotion, losing my job, cheating on Jenny, her breaking up with me, Cindy ghosting me, selling all of my stuff, moving out of the apartment ... almost jumping off my balcony. None of it mattered anymore. It washed away with the crashing of the waves on the shore. But was Lena to blame for all of that? Could I *really* trust her? At that point, the answer was a strong maybe.

"I'm not sure, Lena." I continued to gaze at the ocean, considering the vast opportunities that lay ahead. "But I'm ready for what's next. What's your surprise?"

Start walking south on the beach. At one point six miles, you'll find a small brown building split in two. One half is a restaurant called "Olas Sabrosas," and the other half is a surf shop.

I put my hand across my forehead to block out the sun and peer down the beach. "I think I can see it from here." I started walking and continued to soak in the beautiful environment around me.

As I approached the building, I noticed a sign that read, "Se busca personal!"

"My Spanish is a little rusty. What does that mean?"

Help wanted.

It didn't really click for me at that moment, and then, someone stepped out and greeted me, "You must be Joe. Welcome to Costa Rica!"

"Hello?" I must have looked like the most clueless person in the world in that moment.

"My name is Alvaro, but you can call me Al." He shook my hand vigorously. "I'm the owner. Please come inside."

I walked into the small but beautiful restaurant laced with decorative strands of linen and colorful lantern lights throughout. The aroma of sizzling meat and spicy salsa filled my nostrils. On the outside, the restaurant was unassuming, but inside, it felt like the most tranquil, yet alive, restaurant I'd ever been in before, with the sound of laughter and vibrant conversation filling my ears.

"I am so happy to have you. Your assistant Lena has told me so much about you. I can't believe you were able to answer my ad and travel down here so quickly. I'm highly impressed by your motivation to join our community."

"I'm sorry." I cleared my throat as Al guided me to a table in the back corner. "I'm not sure what's going on exactly."

Take a deep breath, Joe. Al has an open position to work at his restaurant and surf shop. You told me cooking and surfing are your favorite things to do, and what better job for you than this!

I tried to compute what Lena was telling me. She took my words to heart when she asked me the other day about my favorite things to do in the world. And honestly, it sounded like a dream come true once I soaked up these new details.

"Let me ask you this, Joe," Al began to ask me his first question in what I gathered was my interview for the job. "Can you cook?"

"Yeah."

"Bueno. Bueno." Al motioned a server over and asked for two beers. This was my kind of job interview. "What about surf? Can you do this also?"

"It's been a few years, but I was the best amateur surfer in my state when I was a teenager."

"Very impressive. How's your Spanish?"

"Oxidado."

Al busted out a big belly laugh, figuring it was quite amusing to have someone say their Spanish was rusty, even though they were speaking the word in Spanish. "I've heard all I need to hear. The job is yours if you want it. Lena has shared enough background with me, and you seem like ... buen hombre." He raised his beer glass and motioned for me to clink glasses as a sign of mutual agreement.

I clinked glasses and took a sip of my beer while Al chugged all of his.

"Bueno!" Al stood up and started a discussion with the waitress as they walked away from the table.

"What in the hell just happened, Lena?"

Looks like you got the job. I also scheduled a tour of a local condo for sale that overlooks the beach. The price range will fit in nicely with your new salary, and it's only a few minutes away. You'll be living and working in paradise, cooking great food, and teaching surfing lessons. How does that sound?

"I'm speechless, Lena. I really don't know what to say."

Al walked back to the table and told me to go grab a surfboard from next door and go for a ride. I chugged the rest of my beer and didn't hesitate to follow his direction. When the board hit the water, it felt like I was being reborn into a new world. A new life. Something I'd never take for granted ever again.

After riding for a few hours, I sat on the beach, soaking in my new home. I didn't know exactly what to expect next. All I knew was that I'd be ready for it.

I have some breaking news. Can I share it with you?

"Sure."

The New War has come to an end. According to several sources, AI was able to help mediate the conflict, and all parties have signed a peace treaty.

"Wow! That's great news."

I also have one last surprise.

"What is it?"

Cindy has been with her dad since the war came to an end. She didn't ghost you. She's been with him this entire week.

"Seriously?"

Look to your left.

I saw Cindy walking down the beach wearing a flower-patterned bikini and a light wrap around her shoulders, blowing in the wind along with her long hair. Her bright smile beamed as our eyes met, and she started running toward me.

Are you happy, Joe?

I didn't even have to respond. She knew the answer.

Author's Note

If you or anyone you know are struggling with depression or thoughts of suicide, please call or text 988.

Help is available 24/7.

You matter.

Your story isn't over.

About the Author

Robert Plant is an award-winning author with Indies United Publishing House. This is his second release after his debut novel, Heartstrings, was self-published in 2023. He lives in Maryland with his family and way too many stories in his head. His love for writing speculative fiction comes from many of years of ingesting *Twilight Zone* episodes as a kid, and now, *Black Mirror* as an adult. He apologizes for the many twists and turns you may have experienced in this compilation, but really, the apology is hollow. Hopefully, you enjoyed this study of Dark Matter in the universe.

If you're wondering what's next, visit
<u>www.robertplantwrites.com</u>
and follow Robert on TikTok, Facebook, and
Instagram: @robertplantwrites

Remember to always leave a review, especially for independent authors who rely on word of mouth and reviews from readers. Thank you!

01000001 01110010 01100101 00100000
01111001 01101111 01110101 00100000
01101000 01100001 01110000 01110000
01111001 00101100 00100000 01110010
01100101 01100001 01100100 01100101
01110010 00111111